Dane Thorburn
and the
Brindabeare Knights

By Matt Galanos

A catalogue record for this book is available from the National Library of Australia

Publisher:

ASPG (Australian Self Publishing Group)
P.O. Box 159, Calwell, ACT Australia 2905
Email: publishaspg@gmail.com
http://www.inspiringpublishers.com

National Library of Australia Cataloguing-in-Publication entry

Author: Galanos, Matt

Title: **Dane Thorburn and the Brindabeare Knights** / *Matt Galanos*

978-1-925908-14-5 (print)
978-1-925908-15-2 (eBook)

*For Caroline, Melissa
and Michael*

Chapter 1

Betrayal

The evening patrols settled in for their shifts, those manning the perimeter of Brindabeare resigned to the wind and driving rain. Huddled together in drenched overcoats, they scanned the horizon for movement. No one would be able to get within a mile of the great city gates without being spotted and halted under the threat of attack.

Up in the castle, the Royal Knights were on duty - Brindabeare's best, and the sworn protectors of the royal family.

Brindabeare had ruled Valentaland for over three hundred years, since the end of the Great War. Its defences had been built to the point where it was almost impregnable from anything beyond its walls.

However, a betrayal from within was another matter entirely.

✦ ✦ ✦

'Can we play yet?' the boy asks for the umpteenth time.

'In a moment,' his mother sighs.

'Let's go and play without her,' he says to the girl. 'She'll be ages.'

The boy's mother watches as they slip away from the table.

'No wandering off, you two!' she calls. 'If you're not in Vanessa's room when I get there, there'll be trouble.'

They round the corner at the end of the dining hall and break into a run.

They race to the bedroom, a couple of floors up.

'I won!' the young girl exclaims. 'That means I get to hide first!'

'It's my turn!' the boy demands. 'And if I don't go first I'm not playing at all!'

She's counting and he's out the door, sprinting towards the hiding place he'd found just yesterday.

He glances over his shoulder.

She'll never find me, he thinks.

He rounds the bend.

His legs go from under him.

CRASH!

He slams head-first into the floor.

He's dazed and confused.

He untangles himself and stands up.

There's a terrible pain in his chin.

His face is bleeding.

Lifeless bodies litter the hallway.

In a panic he runs, cutting a trail through the wreckage.

He reaches the end of the hallway.

He hears voices.

'All done here, My Lord,' says the first.

It's nasty - it scares the boy senseless.

'Good,' the second replies. 'Go back and seal it off.'

The light entered the room.

Dane and Vanessa gasped.

It was coming from the hand of Lord Frederick. He walked into the room with his hand in front of him, a white light shining out to allow him to see a short distance ahead.

Standing in the middle of the room, it cast an eerie glow around him, making him appear almost surreal. As always, he wore his multi-coloured Masterlord's cape, and Scarafuse, his powerful sword, was at his side.

With Raegan outlawed and unseen since his failed coup, Lord Frederick was the last of the living descendants of the wizards from the ancient city of Nadensa. His Masterlord talent was rare among wizards; and as High Governor he was the most important person in the city after the King.

Dane relaxed a little, relieved it was Lord Frederick, but wary of being found.

With a flick of his hand, Lord Frederick lit all the torches in the room.

'You may come out now,' he said.

Dane was stunned. How did Lord Frederick know they were there? He struggled out from the ledge and helped Vanessa down.

'Lord Frederick,' she began, 'I can explain —'

'It was my idea,' Dane interrupted, 'I found the passageway - I thought nobody knew about it - so I told Vanessa we could practise down here.'

Lord Frederick turned to face them.

'I am not bothered you have used this room,' he replied. 'I have known for some time.'

Seeing their shocked faces, he nodded.

'The middle of last spring - if I am not mistaken.'

Dane and Vanessa exchanged glances; ruing the fact their 'secret room' was no secret at all.

'Aside from the King and myself, there are no others who know it is here.'

Vanessa let out a sigh of relief.

'We're sorry,' she said. 'Please don't tell father or mother. I just wanted a place where Dane and I could practise.'

'I have no intention of saying anything to anyone,' said Lord Frederick. 'However, I am afraid you can no longer make use of this room.'

Relieved, yet disappointed, Vanessa nodded. Dane turned to Lord Frederick with a puzzled look on his face.

'Yes, Master Dane?'

'If you knew we'd been here all this time, why did you wait so long to find us?'

'When I sensed your presence I was interested to know your purpose in being here. Watching your activities, I have been impressed with your teaching, and the ability displayed by the Princess.'

'How have you watched us?' asked Vanessa.

'Wizards have ways, Princess. But I say again. You cannot come here any longer; nor can you reveal the location to anyone. It is critical to Brindabeare and Valentaland it remains hidden.'

'I promise,' said Dane.

'Me too,' said Vanessa.

'Very well,' Lord Frederick replied. 'However, there is no need for the Princess' tutoring to cease.'

'Where can we go?' asked Dane. 'We need somewhere where no-one will interrupt us.'

Lord Frederick smiled.

'You are two of the most resourceful people in Brindabeare, and I am sure there are others who know of this 'arrangement' you have. That alone should guarantee you will find another location.'

He turned to Vanessa, a hint of admiration in his voice. 'How else would you be able to leave your quarters and wander the hallways unchecked, without coming up with one ruse after another to fool at least three maids and five Royal Knights as to your real whereabouts?'

Dane and Vanessa blushed.

'I for one would not have the conscience to do it,' added Lord Frederick, shaking his head. 'Heaven forbid if there was an urgent need to find you. The consequences would be severe, given their livelihoods depend on knowing exactly that.'

Dane felt as though he'd been hit with a sledgehammer. Vanessa gasped.

'We're sorry,' they said in unison.

Lord Frederick laughed.

'You owe me no apology. However, I suggest you find a more practical solution.'

Dane and Vanessa nodded in agreement.

'It may surprise you how willing others are to assist,' Lord Frederick added with a smile.

Dane grinned.

'Your quarters tomorrow morning?' he asked. 'For...advanced history lessons?'

Lord Frederick raised an eyebrow.

Dane hesitated.

'Er, well, how about remedial history for me, and advanced history for Vanessa?'

Lord Frederick chuckled.

'Much better.'

Chapter 3

Too Little Time

'**L**indstrom, can we hurry?' Dane pleaded, glancing out the window. 'If we don't finish soon there won't be any time for riding.'

'Don't be so impatient, young man. The study of history requires concentration. There is nothing to be gained by rushing through it.'

'But you've told us about the Great War so many times. Why do we have to hear it again?'

'The consequences of Edan delving to the very core of the Fire Element are worth repeating, and best understood when I can do so without interruption.'

Lindstrom started re-arranging the battle-board at the front of the room; one of several enchanted walls in the castle created to show mock-battles.

Dane groaned. He could see across the open plain from where he was; but the longer he was forced to sit there, gnashing his teeth in frustration, the more likely he'd miss today's ride.

Edan and the Fire-Walkers, Vrenin's wrath, Nadensa's destruction, Brindabeare's triumph – he'd heard it all before.

Lessons were such a waste! Why be cooped up in a room all day, when you could be outside, in the clean, open air, riding with the wind in your face, without a care in the world? He could feel it, smell it, almost taste it.

'Master Thorburn, your answer please.'

'Huh?'

Dane snapped his head around and found Vanessa and Lindstrom staring at him.

A member of the Brindabeare Council, one of Reginald Lindstrom's many tasks was to serve as Royal Tutor. Dane and Vanessa were his only students (a privilege they both questioned at times), and Dane's constant lapses in concentration were a never-ending source of frustration.

He looked at Vanessa, hoping for a clue.

'No hints, Princess,' said Lindstrom. 'Master Thorburn can answer for himself.'

Helpless, Dane looked at the battle-board, his parchment, and the books lining the wall, hoping the answer would somehow materialise before him.

'I don't know,' he said in a low voice.

'I see,' said Lindstrom, pacing the room. 'You don't know, or you weren't paying attention?'

Not wanting to admit he wasn't listening, Dane meekly chose the first option.

'I see,' said Lindstrom, stopping in front of Dane's desk. 'Brindabeare defeats Candahorn and ends the Great War – and you don't know the name of the man who led us? I find that hard to believe.'

Dane's jaw dropped. Of course he knew! Everyone in Valentaland knew that.

'Malcolm!' he spluttered. 'King Malcolm.'

He looked at Lindstrom, hopeful he'd saved himself, but to no avail. Knowing he'd been caught, he braced himself for what he knew was coming.

'You haven't heard a word I've said,' said Lindstrom. 'So I will extend the lesson while I repeat the last part of this battle. I suggest you give your undivided attention if you wish to leave before the gates are closed.'

Dane's anger raged inside him. Embarrassed at the dressing down he'd received and steaming at the ever-shortening time left to ride, he was tempted to unleash a tirade in Lindstrom's direction. Only a reassuring pat on the shoulder, followed by a gentle, yet pleading shake of the head from Vanessa stopped him.

'However,' his tormentor went on, 'there is no need for others to pay for your indiscretions. Princess, you are dismissed.'

Dane's blood boiled.

'But —'

'Another word and you will be here until sundown,' said Lindstrom.

Slamming his fist on the desk, Dane looked defiantly at Lindstrom. Any chance for a ride was lost, and he knew Lindstrom would enjoy seeing him suffer while he recounted the end of the Great War for the umpteen-hundredth time.

Making her way from the room, Vanessa bumped Dane's chair, dropping her belongings onto the floor. Dane reached down to help. Vanessa winked at him and smiled. Dane smiled back. He'd have time to ride after all.

Halfway through Lindstrom's recital of Brindabeare's victory in the Great War, Dane's mother appeared, right on cue.

'The Princess would like Dane to accompany her on a ride before the evening meal,' said Mistress Marilena Thorburn with a gentle smile. She knew this interruption had been planned but played along, doing her best to portray no knowledge of a plot.

'Very well,' Lindstrom sighed in response. 'Master Thorburn, you may go.'

Dane smiled at Marilena and gathered his things.

'Thank you,' he mouthed.

Marilena nodded.

'Master Thorburn, I would like to offer a word of advice,' said Lindstrom.

'Yes?'

'If you spend more time learning and less complaining, you may find there is more free time at the end of the day.'

'Well – er – thanks,' Dane muttered, winking at Marilena and bolting from the room.

Racing down the stairway, he caught Lindstrom's voice in the background.

'Such potential. A brilliant mind, if only he used it productively.'

The Royal Stables were at the back of the castle. A walkway split the stalls into two rows of five, with riding gear stored in racks at the rear.

Led by a stablehand, Dane's young black colt tossed his head excitedly, stamping his foot in anticipation of what lay ahead.

'I'm glad he's yours Master Dane - he's too feisty for me.'

'Easy, Thunder,' said Dane, taking the reins. The colt calmed immediately, nuzzling against his master.

Vanessa's mount was a chestnut named Buttons she'd ridden for years.

Mounting up they walked the horses towards the castle's main gate. A couple of Royal Knights followed; near enough to be by their side at a moment's notice.

They made their way through the gatehouse and into the city proper, heading down Main Street, a large, wide road that ran the entire length of the city.

People rushed from their homes to wave and watch them pass; young children yelled to each other, running alongside for a moment before falling behind. Vanessa waved back while Dane kept a watchful eye on everything around them.

They passed through the Main Gatehouse, and after crossing the Borsan River Bridge the Royal Knights rode ahead and fanned out to the sides of the open plain. Spurring their mounts on, Dane and Vanessa took flight towards the Great Forest Clearing.

Dane had been in the forest many times and knew the main roads as well as the knights who patrolled it, but it wasn't safe to ride in at their leisure. The clearing was as far as they could go.

Given free rein, Thunder covered the ground with great speed, opening a huge lead by the time they reached the clearing. Dane eased up on the ride back yet still won easily.

Vanessa brought Buttons around to the starting point.

'I think you can give me a ten-count this time.'

'Ten?' said Dane in mock alarm. 'That's not fair. How about five? He's just a colt.'

'And he's knight-bred - the biggest, strongest and fastest we have. Buttons is an ordinary mare, built for comfort, not speed. With a five-count you'll catch me in no time.'

'Very well.'

'No cheating!'

Dane waited, doing his best not to count too fast. With a flick of his wrists, Thunder shot off after the Princess. Every ounce of their combined energy was focused on the mount in front.

No slouch on horseback either, Vanessa reached the clearing first. Turning for home, Dane spurred Thunder hard. Gaining with every stride, the result was in doubt until he stormed into the lead on the last furlong.

'Great ride!' said Dane. 'Ready to go again?'

Before Vanessa could reply they heard the sound of trumpets.

Dane groaned.

'Already?'

'Come on,' said Vanessa, turning Buttons towards the city, 'we have to go.'

Dane looked towards the forest and saw half a dozen riders stream-ing towards them.

'We need to get here earlier,' he said, shaking his head.

'You need to stop complaining during lessons,' Vanessa teased.

Dane grunted in frustration, cursing Lindstrom under his breath as the trumpets rang out once more.

Chapter 4

A Private Battle

The weeks went on and Dane continued to struggle through lessons. Adding to his frustration was how soon the trumpets called them back to the city each day.

'I don't understand it,' he lamented one afternoon. 'When you wish time would pass quickly it never does; but when you're having fun it passes in an instant.'

'Apply yourself and stop thinking about what you may be missing,' said Vanessa. 'You'll be surprised how quickly lessons can finish.'

'You sound like Lindstrom,' said Dane. 'The battles are interesting but the rest is boring. Especially the history of Nadensa and the wizards. It was so long ago.'

'It's all important,' Vanessa countered. 'The destruction of Nadensa was the most tragic event in our history. The wizards were nearly wiped out - *we* were nearly wiped out. If not for King Malcolm, we may have lost everything.'

'What about all the stuff about the Ruling Elements?' said Dane. 'Who cares if so-and-so was a Firelord or a Waterlord? We have Lord Frederick; he's a Masterlord - a Lord in *all* the Ruling Elements.'

'Being a Masterlord doesn't mean you know everything about the Ruling Elements. Lord Frederick said Raegan has a better knowledge of the Fire Element than he does - especially the dark side. That makes him dangerous. The Ruling Elements affect each wizard differently. No two are ever the same.'

'But who cares who knew what over three hundred years ago?'

'I'm sure Lord Frederick would be pleased to hear how little you think of his ancestors.'

'That's not fair!' Dane bristled. 'I may find the lessons boring but that doesn't mean I don't care about Lord Frederick!'

'I know. But one day I'll have to make decisions that affect everyone. Not just Brindabeare, but the whole of Valentaland. I can't do that without learning as much as I can – about everything I can. Sometimes the smallest things help the most.'

'But on a day like this it's such a waste. Wouldn't you rather be riding – or sparring – instead of stuck in a classroom?'

'Wait until you start training,' Vanessa countered. 'They'll ride you so hard you'll be pleading for a break.'

Dane laughed.

'No amount of riding would ever be too much for me.'

'Don't tell me you weren't warned. And you know about Officer Parnsworth - he's a tyrant.'

Marilena appeared at the stables.

'Princess, the Queen has requested your presence before the evening meal.'

The ladies left. Now alone in the stables, Dane continued to pack away the saddles and tend the horses. Not long after, the doors swung open and three youths Dane's age entered.

'What do we have here?' sneered Martin Fenwick. Fenwick was slightly shorter than Dane, with a thin, weasel-like face and shifty, sneaky eyes.

'Her Highness' personal escort has to tend her horses and clean her stable? It must be hard work tending her every need, especially with his mother watching.'

The other two, Vincent Winslow and Austin Harrop, laughed a little too loudly.

Fenwick and Dane had had a mutual dislike for each other since childhood. The young Fenwick had stolen some trinkets from a peddler, and when Dane refused to help cover it up, he'd sworn Dane would pay.

Dane had lost count of the number of times Fenwick had tried to see him humiliated or embarrassed in one way or another. Just last week a lady approached him at market, asking him to look after her horse, only for Fenwick to appear and accuse him of stealing it.

Winslow and Harrop were Fenwick's only known friends, considered by most to be little more than hired thugs. Tall and thickset, they were always on hand to help Fenwick carry out his plans.

Most of the time Dane was able to steer clear of them. He wasn't afraid; it was just better to avoid a three-on-one confrontation if he could. On this occasion there was nothing he could do – they'd staked him out and waited for the opportunity.

'Got anything to say for yourself – or do you need the Princess' permission before you can speak?' Fenwick snorted.

Winslow and Harrop edged forward.

'I have better things to do right now,' Dane replied, doing his best to ignore them.

'I think not.'

They closed in around him.

'Maybe I can change your mind,' said Fenwick, seizing the feed bucket and throwing the contents all over the floor.

In the same instant Winslow and Harrop lunged at Dane, trying to pin him against the stable wall. Moving quickly, Dane turned around and caught Winslow with an elbow to the head. Winslow went howling to the ground. Harrop had a firm hold of Dane's other hand and was trying to land a blow of his own.

They spun around, struggling, and Dane was about to break free when he was confronted by Fenwick; sword out, holding it to Dane's face.

'No you don't,' he said, moving in and jabbing Dane's chest with the blade. 'I can't stand violence and bloodshed; especially in the Royal Stables - it just won't do.'

Harrop grabbed Dane's hands and pinned them behind his back. A couple of stablehands appeared. Although helpless in Harrop's grip, Dane shook his head and they reluctantly slunk away.

'It's time you were put back where you belong,' said Fenwick, poking Dane with his sword. 'I've had enough of seeing you get special privileges and strut around like a peacock. I'm a better escort for the Princess than you'll ever be. It should be me - not you.'

'Not a chance,' Dane spat, struggling under Harrop's grasp. 'I see you can't do anything without your hired help doing all the dirty work.'

Fenwick leaned forward and stood eye-to-eye with Dane.

'Not a good idea to be disrespectful when you're defenseless,' he replied, dropping his sword and punching Dane hard in the stomach.

Dane collapsed to the ground, catching a boot in the chest as he went down.

'Wait till we get to training!' snarled Fenwick, a second kick finding its mark. 'Then the Princess will see what a pathetic excuse for a knight you really are!'

He gave Dane one last kick - to the face this time. He turned to leave, laughed and added, 'and clean up this mess! We can't have all this feed all over the floor now, can we?'

Winslow and Harrop couldn't resist the chance to lay their boots into Dane on their way out.

Dane was a mess. He was winded, bruised, and his clothes were torn.

Night had fallen by the time he'd finished cleaning the stable and restored his appearance to something resembling his normal self, but didn't feel any better when he arrived at the castle.

He entered the Great Dining Hall, trying to be as inconspicuous as possible.

'What on earth happened to you!?' Marilena exclaimed.

The entire room turned to face him.

'Nothing,' Dane replied, taking his seat and doing his best not to wince in pain. 'Trouble with the horses. Thunder kicked me and knocked his feed everywhere. When I was cleaning it up he kicked me again.'

'But he's fully trained!' Marilena said with disbelief. 'And how did you cut your face?'

Dane felt his anger rising.

'When I was kicked,' he said, struggling to control his emotions. 'May I have some meat please?' he asked, trying to change the subject.

The other diners looked on with varying degrees of interest. At the head of the table sat King Winston and Queen Olivia. To the King's right and the Queen's left sat their aides, Harold Salsbury and Patrice Whiltshire.

Lord Frederick and Lindstrom were there, along with the other members of the Brindabeare Council, Maurice Fairbrother and Patrick Medhurst. Also dining tonight were two guests: General Laramer Silvers, Commander-in-Chief of the Brindabeare Army, and Officer Ronald Parnsworth, the Cadet Training Commander.

The evening meal was always lavish, with plenty of meats, cheeses and fruits to choose from. An array of wines were on offer, along with cider for Dane and Vanessa. Servants fussed about and Royal Knights guarded the entrances.

A huge replica of the Brindabeare Coat of Arms hung from the wall behind the King and Queen; imposing itself on proceedings in the glare of the evening torches around it.

No one said anything more to Dane about his appearance; but Vanessa and Marilena cast suspicious eyes at him, and he heard Silvers, Medhurst and Parnsworth exchange views about the story he'd concocted.

'Kicked by his own horse!?' Silvers observed to Parnsworth. 'And we trust him to escort the Princess?' He shook his head in disgust. 'He won't last long in training.'

'I think he'd make it through the first session and be ready to come home with his tail between his legs,' Parnsworth chortled.

'Doesn't look the knight type, really,' added Medhurst. 'If he were anyone else, I wouldn't give him the time of day.'

'Don't know about his ability with a sword either,' said Parnsworth. 'It's hard to believe he's Gil Thorburn's son.'

The others nodded.

'Gentlemen, I think there's something you've failed to notice,' said Maurice Fairbrother. 'If you look closely, you'll notice a bruise on Master Thorburn's face, just under his right eye.'

They glanced at Dane for a moment, before Fairbrother went on. 'If that injury was the result of a horse-kick, he'd be dead.'

'I believe you're right,' Silvers replied.

'It's clear something happened which Master Thorburn does not wish to divulge,' Fairbrother added. 'What may be seen by some as the privileges of his relationship with the Princess places him in a difficult position when dealing with gentlemen his own age.'

Silvers nodded thoughtfully.

'Contrary to being critical, I think it admirable he chose to deal with the matter himself, rather than using his standing among this group to seek retribution. If you ask me, just the type of quality you would want to see in a knight.'

'We'll see whether he possesses the qualities of a knight in a few weeks' time,' Parnsworth concluded. 'Now, that pheasant looks enticing.'

✦ ✦ ✦

Raegan bends down, looking the boy in the eye.

'I am about to become the ruler of Brindabeare,' he says. 'And there is no place for you in my kingdom'...

A flash of red - his father falls to the floor...
'Father!...Father!...Come back!...Come back!'
He kicks.
He screams.
He blacks out.
Dane woke with a jolt. Breathing heavily, he looked around.

It was morning again.

The familiar ache in his chin was there, but today there were throbbing pains in his head, chest, and stomach.

Struggling out of bed, he was late to class.

'Master Thorburn,' said Lindstrom. 'You are aware of our starting time?'

'Yes,' Dane deadpanned in response.

'An explanation please.'

'I don't have one,' Dane answered in the same flat tone. 'I'm sorry I was late.'

Making his way to his seat, he ignored the scowl on Vanessa's face.

'You will make up the time at the end of the day,' said Lindstrom.

When there was no response, Vanessa's mood changed from anger to surprise. Punishment like this usually led to a barrage of complaints, but today there was nothing.

The lesson continued. Dane didn't speak and ignored Vanessa's attempts to gain his attention.

'What's wrong?' she asked when Lindstrom left the room during their break. 'You missed our sparring session and you've hardly said a word all morning.'

'I'm not feeling well.'

'There's more to it than that. Something's up, and I want to know.'

'I'm sore where I was kicked.'

'I heard Fairbrother talking to Silvers, and the others last night. He said you were covering up what actually happened and I think he's right. Thunder would never kick you. What's going on?'

'I dropped the bucket and he kicked me. It was an accident. I'm sore and it hurts. That's it.'

'Well, if you're going to be like that, then don't expect any sympathy from me,' said Vanessa, irritated at his reluctance to tell the truth.

'I didn't *ask* for sympathy,' Dane hissed, anger boiling inside him.

'Fine!' Vanessa snapped.

'FINE!' Dane yelled, hurling his ink well at the far wall, where it shattered, sending a shower of ink and glass everywhere.

Vanessa looked at Dane, stunned. She couldn't recall the last time he'd lost his temper at her like that. Dane stood still, in a dazed, semi-confused state.

'Sorry,' he said.

'It's alright. I want to help.'

'I know. But some things I need to face on my own.'

'Master Thorburn,' said Lindstrom, re-entering the room, 'you will serve time after class cleaning the mess you have made. I will not tolerate such misbehaviour.'

'Yes, Lindstrom,' Dane answered. This time it was Lindstrom's turn to look surprised.

Halfway through his detention, a familiar scene played itself out and Dane was soon heading to the stables to saddle the horses.

Every muscle in his arms and chest hurt. He threw the saddles on, wincing in pain with each one. Seeing his discomfort, Vanessa hesitated.

'Maybe we shouldn't ride today.'

'No – I want to. I'm not going to let anything stop us doing what we normally do.'

Walking the horses towards the Main Gate, Dane noticed Fenwick, Winslow, and Harrop out of the corner of his eye. Sitting taller in the saddle, he saw a look of surprise, then anger on Fenwick's face. The pain in his body seemed to ease a little. He was also pleased to see Winslow's face was still swollen, an ugly bruise under one eye.

In what seemed like no time at all, Dane and Vanessa headed back to the stables. It had been as good a ride as they'd had in a while. The afternoon sky had been clear, a gentle breeze making the ride pleasant and effortless.

'That was wonderful,' said Vanessa, handing the reins over. 'Sometimes it's as though Buttons and I mould into one being, one flowing force.'

'I know what you mean,' said Dane. 'I feel that way every time I ride.'

Dane started unstrapping the horses.

'How are you feeling now?' Vanessa asked.

'Better. I'm still sore, but they don't know I'm hurt and that's what counts.'

Vanessa didn't really know what he was talking about, but seeing he was happy for the first time that day, she decided not to ask.

Chapter 5
Black Knights

The two met deep in the Great Forest, away from prying eyes, the canopy so thick only slivers of sunlight were visible. Their horses shifted on the spot, unsettled by the lack of light and the forbidding noises around them.

Raegan turned to his companion, 'The Thorburn boy. You know him?'

The man wore black from head to foot, his face smeared with black paint.

'I dine with him on occasion at the castle.'

'His aptitude in military affairs?'

'I'm not sure, My Lord. Once he commences training we will know more.'

'Can he be turned? He trusted me once. Perhaps he could learn to trust me again.'

'No, My Lord. He would never turn against the Princess.'

Raegan considered the man's response.

'Very well. You will monitor him. As the son of Gil Thorburn he is not to be underestimated.'

'My Lord,' said the other man, 'he is just a boy.'

Raegan spoke quietly, as though he was thinking aloud.

'I suspect he possesses many of the qualities so admired in his father. A boy he may be, but if he realises his potential, he may become a threat. I have no desire to see another Thorburn stand in my way.'

The man nodded.

'To other matters,' said Raegan. 'A meeting with the High Command; it is time for an update.'

He closed his eyes, concentrating for a few moments.

'The summons has been sent. Let us proceed to the meeting point.'

The navigation lesson had been particularly gruelling, and when break time arrived, Vanessa decided a walk outside was in order.

'Lindstrom, I'd like a longer break this morning.'

Dane smiled.

'Very well,' Lindstrom sighed. 'You are to be back at the high-point of the sun - understood?'

Once outside they headed to a clearing near the Mill Gate, chatting about the morning's lesson.

'You know what would be really interesting?' Dane asked.

'What?'

'Mapping the Astuvius Falls. It's never been done. Who knows, you may even find Seruza.'

'That's a rumour,' said Vanessa. 'And she's the Goddess of Water! If she lived there she'd sense you from miles away. You won't find any of the gods unless they want to be found. Wizard, witch, man or woman – no one's ever seen any of them.'

'What about Vrenin? He wiped out the Fire-Walkers and nearly everything else at the height of the Great War. Everyone says it was his wrath that did it. Someone must have seen him - the God of Fire in all his fury.'

'Remember what Lindstrom said? The wrath of Vrenin was unleashed from *somewhere* within the Highland Mountains. Vrenin was never seen, and the few who went looking never came back.'

'Wouldn't it be good, though?' Dane grinned. 'If we found him and asked about the Great War? How Edan penetrated the Fire Element and created the Fire-Walkers. It would sure put Lindstrom in his place.'

Vanessa laughed.

'Now you're being ridiculous.'

'I know. But think about it. We'd never have to sit through hearing it from Lindstrom ever again.'

'Well,' said Vanessa, returning his smile, 'it's an interesting proposition.'

Starting back towards the castle, they heard a panicked voice behind them.

'Princess! Princess!' the man yelled. 'Master Dane! Master Dane!'

The voice belonged to Angus Flitson, the Royal Falconer. He was thought to be mad by most people, but to Vanessa and Dane he was harmless.

'Princess! Master Dane!' he repeated, catching up to them. 'Black Knight in the forest! Reuben saw him, Reuben saw him!'

'Where?' Dane asked. 'When?'

'In the forest, Master Dane! In the forest!'

'When?' Dane asked again.

'Reuben saw him Master Dane! Reuben saw him!'

'Angus, calm down,' Dane replied. 'We'll help you. But you need to calm down.'

Angus relaxed a little.

'Are you sure Reuben saw a Black Knight?'

'Yes, Master Dane. He told me himself. Reuben saw a Black Knight.'

'Did he say where?'

'In the Great Forest, Master Dane,' Angus replied, pointing wildly. 'In the Great Forest. Said it was a long way from his house. He can show you. He's an expert in the forest you know. Knows all of it, Reuben does. I'm sure he can show you.'

Dane thought about what to do. If the Black Knight had been seen anywhere near the Brindabeare side of the forest, it would be the nearest sighting since the failed coup.

Raegan hadn't been seen since that night, but his private army of Black Knights had been spotted in varying numbers, wreaking havoc in towns and provinces. Striking in short, sharp bursts, they left a trail of mayhem and destruction.

The size of his army was unknown, but everyone knew men throughout the land had been recruited to join them. The extent of the Black Knight network was revealed when Lord Frederick discovered that Middleton, one of Brindabeare's most senior Royal Knights, was a Black Knight.

From that point there was always a question lurking below the surface, no matter how trusting a man appeared – could he be a Black Knight?

News of their activities created an undercurrent of suspicion and tension among the people, and the King had a network of spies deployed throughout the land, seeking information as to where they might strike next.

Vanessa broke the silence.

'We have to get to Reuben and find out what we can.' She thought for a moment, then her mind was clear. 'Dane, you have to go.'

'What?' Dane asked in disbelief. 'Now?'

'Now. No one will believe Angus, and they won't believe Reuben either. But they might believe you.'

Speechless for a moment, Dane knew Vanessa was right. The only way to establish credibility to what Angus was saying was to find out himself.

'Very well,' he replied. 'Angus, I need your horse.'

'Of course Master Dane! Anything you ask. Anything at all.'

One of the Royal Knights guarding Vanessa approached.

'Is everything alright here?' he asked. 'Where are you going Master Thorburn?'

'I'm....er....going to retrieve a pack that Angus left in the forest,' Dane replied, doing his best to sound convincing. 'He's frightened because he dropped it. Isn't that right, Angus?'

'Yes yes yes!' Angus replied, nodding and pointing wildly.

The Royal Knight hesitated.

'Do you wish me to escort you?'

'No,' Dane replied. 'I'll be fine. Really.'

'If you're not back when the shadow crosses the bridge I'll be coming after you.'

Dane nodded. Vanessa breathed a sigh of relief.

'You and Angus wait here,' said Dane, turning towards the forest. 'I'll be back as soon as I can.'

Reuben's cave was well hidden. Built to blend with the landscape and reflect the light and shade of the surrounding area, it played tricks on the untrained eye. If you didn't know what you were looking at you'd ride past without a second thought.

Reuben was a scuttler, three feet tall, slightly hunched over, with a narrow, rodent-like face and large green eyes. His furry skin was completely grey, and he was dressed in his latest combination of rags.

Scuttlers were forest foragers, hoarders of whatever they found, useful and useless alike. If space became cramped they would dig out more of the cave to make room. Throwing anything away was unspeakable; scuttlers fight to the death to protect their belongings.

A portal was hidden nearby; the means by which they travelled to the location of any of their kind.

Considered a nuisance by most people, scuttlers normally kept to themselves. Dane and Vanessa befriended Reuben on a trip to the forest with Lord Frederick a couple of years ago.

'Master Dane, what brings you here?'

'Greetings, Reuben, I need some information,' said Dane. 'And I brought you this,' he added, handing over a rock he'd picked up near the Mill Gate.

Reuben's eyes widened as he took it.

'A wonderful treasure!' he remarked, studying it as though it were a priceless diamond. 'Thank you Master Dane. What do you need to know?'

'Angus told me you saw a Black Knight. Is this true?'

Reuben nodded.

'A while ago. Rode right past me. I was at Manfred's portal.'

'How many?'

'Just one.'

'Just one? Are you sure?'

Reuben nodded.

'You didn't hear or see any others? They're usually in groups.'

'I only saw one,' said Reuben.

'Which way was he going?'

'Towards Brindabeare. I saw Angus and told him what I saw.'

'Thank you, Reuben,' said Dane, shaking his hand. 'I have to get back.'

'Goodbye, Master Dane,' Reuben said with a bow. 'Thank you again for the treasure.'

Dane untied Angus' horse and was about to mount up when a noise distracted him.

About thirty feet away, directly in his line of sight a horse shuddered to a halt. Dane watched the rider dismount. He wore Brindabeare armour, but Dane couldn't see who it was.

The man stepped away from his mount and held out his arms, tilting his head slightly. His body shivered from head to foot. At the same time, from the ground up, the man's armour changed; from the Brindabeare silver to black — feet, leggings, chestplate, gauntlets and gloves.

The man turned, absorbing the effect of his transformation. His face was blacked out, a layer of bodypaint masking his identity. He looked larger and stronger than before - the well-known result of the increase in strength Raegan's men experienced from the dark side of the fire element.

Dane rocked back - a Black Knight - right in front of him!

There was another noise and four more horses arrived. Three of the riders were Black Knights. Dane couldn't believe his eyes.

Something big was brewing, and when he saw the last rider he knew it was momentous. He was dressed in black and wore a red cape.

Dane froze.

Images of eleven years ago flashed through his mind, and for an instant he was five years old again: standing in the hallway, paralysed with fear, looking into the face of the wizard who was about to kill him.

Chapter 6
Before The Council

Dane stood there, unable to move. Other images of eleven years ago raced through his mind – stumbling in the hallway; his father falling, his terrified scream.

Sweat dripped down his face.

Wiping his eyes, he looked at Raegan again...

The view was the same, but the image was different. Like a fog lifting to reveal a clear day, he now saw Raegan through his own eyes - this wasn't a dream – it was real.

Instead of fear he felt resentment – a *hatred* towards Raegan for the first time. He wasn't going to scream and run; he was going to do something to help rid Brindabeare of this evil.

It would be a risk – but if he could get closer he'd be able to hear what they were saying. Maybe something the King and Lord Frederick could use to their advantage.

He moved out of view of the five men. Leaving the horse within reach, he edged forward, finding shelter behind a clump of bushes.

'We are not yet ready to move,' he heard one Black Knight say.

'You don't think they're prepared for an attack?' asked another.

'They're so well defended,' replied the first, 'not to mention the problem of Lord Frederick.'

Raegan cut them off.

'Gentlemen. Your observations are noted. However, I do not believe an attack can be executed at this time. We will be in a better position once this charade plays out.'

Five sets of eyes were locked on Raegan; five sets of ears hanging on every word.

'Before we can attack the city directly, we will need an event, a distraction, where they will be unaware of the wider scheme.'

Dane had heard enough. It was clear – Raegan was planning to attack Brindabeare! He had to get back and warn them.

Edging away from the group, he retraced his steps.

'I think I know how —' said Raegan, stopping mid-sentence and raising his hand.

He listened, he looked.

Nothing.

He listened again.

Chirp, chirp, *tap*.

And again.

Chirp, chirp, *tap*.

What was that sound?

He raised his hand in the direction of the strange noise.

A green light shot out, popping in the air directly above Angus' horse, which had been stamping its hoof on the ground.

Raegan saw it immediately, and a moment later a figure emerged from the bushes.

'There!' he yelled. 'Over there!'

The Black Knights charged.

A ray of bright red pierced the air, slamming into a tree inches from Dane's head.

Dane leapt aboard the horse and kicked hard. He had a start on them, but knew they'd outflank him and cut him off before he reached the clearing.

'Over here!' shouted one.

'On my left!' shouted another.

He heard the sound of horses in pursuit, gaining with every stride. Looking over his shoulder, he narrowly missed an overhanging branch, catching a mouthful of leaves. Tearing it away, he urged his mount on, riding for his life.

'We've got him now!' shouted the first Black Knight. Dane could hear him racing ahead, in front to his left. Another was in a similar position to his right. The other two, still behind him, were getting closer; swords out, ready for the kill.

Glancing over his shoulder, the golden tip on one of the swords caught the sun, reflecting into his face and blinding him for a moment.

Thinking he'd been hit by some kind of spell, he turned away. Squinting the light from his eyes, he urged his mount on.

There was no escape.

He was outmaneuvered, and when they converged he'd have nowhere to go. Drawing his sword, he prepared for the inevitable.

Out of nowhere, with a loud *crack!* a large tree collapsed to his right. He heard the anguished squeal of a horse forced to stop dead in its tracks. There was another loud *crack!* and a crash to his left. A second tree went down, forcing the other rider ahead of him to veer sharply off course.

Stunned at his good fortune, he rode on.

The edge of the forest and the open plain to Brindabeare loomed ahead. Glancing over his shoulder, he saw the two giving chase weren't as close as before. Looking again he saw they were slowing down.

What was going on? They'd nearly caught him and now they were giving up. It didn't make sense.

He rode on, slowing down when he reached the clearing. An idea crossed his mind – maybe they didn't want to be seen. If they'd chased any further they might have run into a patrol.

But the others – how did that happen?

Flustered and confused, he started towards the Mill Gate when a voice spoke right next to him.

'Are you alright Master Dane?'

Dane turned around.

'Lord Frederick?' he asked in surprise. 'How did you get here?'

'Reuben found me. The scuttler network is very efficient in these situations. Reuben told me of your predicament and I materialised immediately. Just in time to stop the Black Knights surrounding you.'

'That was you?'

Lord Frederick nodded.

'I slowed one rider, which appeared to be enough to stop them all.'

Dane was puzzled.

'But – two trees fell.'

Lord Frederick raised an eyebrow, then brushed the thought away with a wave of his hand.

'No matter. We need to get back to the castle. Do you mind if I ride with you?'

Vanessa thought she was seeing things when she saw Lord Frederick with Dane. Angus went wide-eyed with shock. Vanessa's guards moved closer, ready to whisk her away.

'Lord Frederick! What's wrong?' she asked. 'What are you doing with Dane?'

Lord Frederick raised his hand.

'It's alright, Princess. I cannot discuss it here. We need to interrupt the Leader's Conference and convene an emergency meeting of the Council.'

Vanessa's eyes widened. Dane and Lord Frederick dismounted.

'Thanks, Angus,' said Dane, handing over the reins.

'Angus, not a word to anyone,' said Lord Frederick, holding a finger to his lips.

'No, Lord Frederick,' Angus replied bowing, 'not a word to anyone.'

'All of you,' said Lord Frederick, looking at the Royal Knights. 'I have not been seen all day – is that clear?'

The Royal Knights nodded.

Lord Frederick dematerialised in a flash of light.

Dane and Vanessa headed towards the castle.

By the time they reached the gatehouse, Dane had recounted his escape twice. Vanessa was stunned.

'Raegan –' she said in disbelief, 'this close to Brindabeare.'

'Shhh!' Dane whispered. 'Others may hear.'

Approaching the castle proper, they heard a patrol stop nearby and dismount. Leading them was General Laramer Silvers, Commander-in-Chief of the Brindabeare Army. Tall and strong, he had the build of the quintessential Royal Knight. Today he walked with a slight limp, but he was an imposing presence just the same.

Dane watched them lead the horses away. A thought struck him - Where were they when he was in the forest? *Four* Black Knights chased him - and the patrol didn't see or hear anything???

'Well well,' said Lindstrom when they arrived back in the South Tower. 'A nice break indeed. Since when does the high-point of the sun leave shadows on this side of the castle?'

'There'll be no more lessons today,' Vanessa replied.

'But Princess –'

'Lord Frederick is organising a Council meeting. Dane's just escaped from four Black Knights and Raegan was with them!'

Lindstrom's jaw dropped. He stood there aghast, not knowing what to say. For a moment he thought this was another of their schemes, but glancing at Dane he saw it was no trick.

'Very – well,' he spluttered. 'Are you coming Master Thorburn?'

'Yes,' Vanessa replied. 'Dane, you have to be there!'

'But - Lord Frederick,' Dane countered. 'He was there too.'

'He helped you escape - but you're the one who saw Raegan.'

They made their way down from the South Tower. Crossing a courtyard, they headed down a stairway on the other side of the castle. Entering the Council waiting room, they were met by Salsbury.

'Master Thorburn, you need to wait here. I'll collect you when the Council is ready. We will be meeting in the smaller chamber today. The Leader's Convention is being held in the main room.'

Dane went over the events again and again in his head. Did he have all his facts right? He'd never appeared before Council before, and the last thing he wanted to do was make a fool of himself.

'Master Thorburn? The Council is ready now.'

The doors to the Council Chamber opened.

The King was at the head of the table, resplendent in full royal attire. Lord Frederick sat to the left, next to Vanessa. Marilena stood behind her. Opposite were Maurice Fairbrother, Patrick Medhurst, and Lindstrom. Salsbury took his place behind the King.

Dane felt uneasy standing alone in the middle of the room. Although he dined with them, apart from Lord Frederick and Lindstrom he'd never met them in an official capacity. He felt their eyes on him, watching his every move.

'Lord Frederick tells me you have news that may interest us,' said the King. 'Please, tell us all.'

'Well Sire, we were near the Mill Gate, when we met Angus —'

'You mean Angus Flitson - that lunatic?' asked Medhurst.

'Yes,' Dane replied, flashing a savage look at Medhurst, 'he told us his friend Reuben, a scuttler, had seen a Black Knight —'

'You mean to say you've interrupted the Leader's Convention to tell us a story passed on by a lunatic and a scuttler?' asked Medhurst.

'Let him finish!' said Vanessa.

'But Princess, surely you're not going to take this seriously?'

'I SAID LET HIM FINISH!' Vanessa yelled, jumping up and slamming her fist on the table.

'Enough!' said the King. 'No one will speak until Master Thorburn has finished.'

Dane continued.

'Reuben said he'd seen a Black Knight – but only one, which I thought was a bit odd. When I was leaving, a noise distracted me. I looked up and saw a Brindabeare Knight stop in front of me. He went into a trance – and turned into a Black Knight.'

'He what!!?' asked Medhurst in disbelief.

'He turned into a Black Knight,' Dane said again. 'From head to toe. I didn't see his face before he transformed, so I don't know who it was. Then three others arrived with Raegan.'

'How did you manage to escape?' asked the King.

Dane glanced at Lord Frederick.

'With Lord Frederick's help. I was surrounded. Lord Frederick stopped the first two and the others gave up. I think I was too close to the edge of the forest and they didn't want to be seen.'

'Quite right,' said Maurice Fairbrother. 'They may have run into a patrol.'

'Actually, I thought that was strange,' Dane replied.

'What do you mean?' asked Fairbrother.

Dane took a deep breath.

Outlining his earlier thoughts about the 'absence' of a patrol, he saw shocked looks appear on a couple of faces around the table.

'Well thought, Master Thorburn,' said Lindstrom with an approving nod. 'It's something we should discuss further.'

'The patrols could have been there all the time,' said Medhurst. 'If Thorburn was riding for his life he wouldn't have had time to examine the scenery.'

'Then why didn't they assist?' Lindstrom shot back.

'Enough,' said the King. 'We will discuss the matter later.'

The room fell silent.

'You're sure the other person was Raegan?' asked the King.

'I'd recognise him anywhere,' said Dane. 'I'll never forget his face.'

The King nodded and glanced at Lord Frederick.

'I think he cast a spell of some kind,' Dane added. 'A light appeared right over my head.'

'A revealing spell,' Medhurst cut in. 'You must have been careless. He must have either seen you or heard you. If you'd been more careful, you would have made a clean getaway, instead of nearly getting yourself killed.'

'I think everything Dane did was incredibly brave!' said Vanessa.

'I agree,' said Lord Frederick, speaking for the first time. Medhurst glowered but said nothing. 'Master Dane,' asked Lord Frederick, 'did you hear anything of their conversation?'

'Yes I did.'

A hush fell around the room. Everyone was quiet, hanging on every word.

'They talked about you, and about not knowing our military strength. How they'd need to create an event, or something that would show them what they needed to know, without us realising it.'

'Anything else?' Lord Frederick asked.

'No,' Dane replied. 'That's it.'

'Leave us to consider these events,' said the King. 'However, before you go, I want it known that Master Thorburn has done a great deed; without fear or favour, or concern for his own well-being. It gives me comfort to know that you may soon be a member of my army. Dismissed.'

Marilena beamed. Vanessa smiled.

'Thank you Sire,' said Dane, bowing himself from the room.

Crossing the courtyard, he couldn't remember a time in his life when he felt better than he did at that moment.

Chapter 7
A Rough First Day

Dane's encounter with Raegan and the Black Knights had far-reaching ramifications. The emergency meeting convened by the King led to uproar at the Leader's Convention.

Insulted by the King's refusal to explain the interruption, the Candahorn delegation, led by their ruler, Governor Randall Mortensen, withdrew their obligations to the Valentaland Charter, declared their intent to establish their independence and stormed out.

Drawn up at the end of the Great War, the Valentaland Charter was renewed by all cities and provinces each year at the Convention. Signing the charter confirmed their ongoing loyalty to Brindabeare and the rule of the King. Despite occasional pockets of trouble and a couple of significant uprisings, it had been largely successful.

As talk of events enveloped the city, Dane found people casting suspicious looks at him.

'They think it's my fault,' he said to Vanessa one afternoon some days later.

'Absolutely not,' she replied. 'Lord Frederick believes it was pre-planned - the Council meeting at the Convention was an excuse.'

'Maybe,' said Dane, unconvinced. 'But if I'd made a clean getaway, none of this would have happened.'

'We've had over three hundred years of peace since the Great War, but Candahorn have never accepted their place as being subservient to Brindabeare. They sign the Charter every year and say all the right things to make people believe they're loyal; but deep down, we've always known they can't be trusted.'

Seeing the uncertainty in Dane's eyes, Vanessa continued.

'Remember, Edan took refuge in Candahorn, used that time to create or awaken the Fire-Walkers, and with Candahorn's help, destroyed all of Nadensa – the ruling city of all the land, and the wizards within it – with the exception of Lord Frederick and Raegan. Having done all this they would have thought victory over Brindabeare and its forces a formality.'

'I know, I know,' said Dane.

'But King Malcolm, Lord Frederick and Raegan, and Vrenin's wrath, or whatever it was, destroyed Edan and the Fire-Walkers, and Brindabeare triumphed.'

'You're sounding like Lindstrom again.'

Taking Dane's hand, Vanessa said gently, yet firmly, 'Dane, Candahorn have wanted to do this for years. Until now they hadn't found a cause that suited their needs. Claiming we insulted them is a reason to say abandoning the Charter is *our* fault. If you weren't the rider in the forest, it would have been someone else.'

'What about the others?' asked Dane.

'Rhondo? Pardosta? Candahorn puppets, both of them. We had suspicions Candahorn were building an alliance. Now we know.'

They were outside the Mill Gate, standing where they'd met Angus the week before. Cadet Training started the next day; this would be their last walk for a while. Compulsory for all males once they turned sixteen, Dane was one of ten who'd be training this year.

'I'm going to miss this,' said Vanessa.

'What?'

'Coming here with you each afternoon and getting away from it all. I'll have to go to tutoring by myself. It won't be the same.'

'We still have weekends.'

'Not really. Father told me I shouldn't show favour.'

'What do you mean?'

'While you're training, I can't be seen to treat you any different to the other cadets.'

'You mean we can't see each other at all?' Dane asked with a hint of anger.

'No. It means it can't be as...visible. I can't ride with you until you finish training. We can see each other, but it has to be inside the castle.'

Dane nodded.

'You may find you're having such a great time that you won't want to see me anyway.'

'You're my best friend,' Vanessa replied. 'I could never think that.'

'I was concerned our friend had done his job too well,' Raegan said to his companion. 'For a moment I thought we were not going to be discovered at all. Then I had to intervene and ensure the rider escaped. Once the convention was disrupted, the rest fell into place.'

'Remind me again – why aren't you concerned about putting them on a war footing?'

'They cannot defend everything at once my friend. When the time comes you will understand.'

The other man nodded.

'I must be away,' said Raegan, extending his hand to the other man. 'Until we meet again.'

Raegan stepped back and dematerialised in a flash of light.

Governor Mortensen looked at the empty space for a moment, then smiled, turned, and walked away.

The next day, after a light breakfast, a kiss from Marilena, and a hug from a slightly teary Princess, Dane gathered all his things and arrived at the Cadet Quarters. He had his sword, shield, knives, quiver with bow and arrows, and his dress armour. He'd already moved Thunder to the Cadet Stables.

The first order of business was to stow their equipment.

The cadets were housed next to the castle, separate from the Royal Knights and the main army. In a war situation, Cadet Quarters served as a marshalling point. All weapons and riding equipment would be checked and sorted there.

The cadets slept in one room, a row of beds lining each wall. Each lodging was large enough to house their belongings comfortably. The room was separated from the stables by a small courtyard.

Making his way inside, Dane felt a sharp prod in his back.

'Now we're here, we'll see what you're really made of.'

It was Fenwick, right behind him; his knife in Dane's back, concealed from view.

Dane reached around to wrench the knife away.

'No you don't,' said Fenwick, twisting the knife and pressing harder. 'We don't want to create a scene now, do we? We'll soon find out who the real Royal Knight is,' he said, pushing past Dane and heading towards his lodging.

Dane boiled but said nothing. He found his lodging and started stowing his weapons, mumbling about what he'd do to Fenwick if they had to fight each other in training.

'You're Dane, aren't you?'

Turning around, Dane saw a face he hadn't seen before.

'I saw what Fenwick did. You'll need to watch him; he's a nasty piece of work. I'm Will. Will Hevenshire.'

Will was slightly shorter and thinner than Dane, with black, wavy hair. His face was flushed, having laboured under the load he had been carrying.

'Thanks Will,' Dane replied, shaking hands. Will didn't seem the least perturbed at knowing who Dane was. At least one friendly face.

They stowed their gear and were ordered outside. Standing before them, resplendent in full Royal Knight battle armour was General Silvers. It was the first time most had seen the General this close and it was an intimidating sight. He towered over them, his armour glinting in the morning light, his eyes fixed straight ahead, boring into them with an intensity that sent a shiver down their spines.

'You are this year's cadets,' he announced in his most rousing pre-battle rallying voice. 'Let me tell you right now, Cadet Training is not for the faint-hearted. It is designed to find out if you have the ability to serve in the Brindabeare Army. It will test your skills to the limit. I do not expect all of you to complete it successfully.

'For those who do not make the grade, there are other ways to earn a living,' he said in a tone that implied any other living was a death sentence.

'For any who possess superior abilities, there is the opportunity to join me, as a member of the Royal Knights.'

An excited murmur rippled up and down the lines of cadets.

'Officer Parnsworth has been instructed to identify anyone worthy of this rank. Those put forward will receive additional training under my personal guidance.'

Dane felt a tingle run down the back of his neck. He wanted nothing more than to be chosen.

'I wish you all the best of luck.' Silvers turned on his heel and strode away.

The cadets stood there, alone, unsure what to do.

Of the group, Dane knew Fenwick, Winslow, Harrop and now Will. The others were Morgan Hainsley, Donovan Braidwood, Henry Featherstone, Hamish Ingham and Albert Webster.

'I think someone should go and see what we're supposed to do,' said Fenwick. 'Go on Thorburn.'

'I'm not going anywhere,' said Dane.

'I think you are!'

Before Dane could react, Winslow and Harrop, standing behind him, grabbed Dane and threw him to the ground.

'Now find someone who'll tell us what to do!' yelled Fenwick.

Dane stood up and turned to face Fenwick.

'I'm not going,' he said again. 'If you're so keen to find out, go and look yourself.'

'I don't think he's listening,' Fenwick replied.

Before he could continue, a loud voice drowned him out.

'What is going on here?!'

Turning around, Dane found himself looking straight at Officer Parnsworth. Parnsworth didn't have the same physical presence as the General, but made up for it in the way he carried himself. A man used to giving orders, he accepted nothing less than exalted obedience.

'Thorburn - who told you to get out of line?' demanded Parnsworth.

Dane hesitated.

'I asked a question and I expect an answer. Who told you to get out of line?'

'Nobody sir,' Dane replied. 'I wasn't out of line, I —'

'You're not out of line? Then why are there two lines behind you with a space where you're supposed to be?!'

'But sir, I was p —'

'Enough! No one told you to move from your place, but you seem to think you're above the rules. So let me tell you something right now. I am in charge. I will tell you what to do and when to do it. For your insolence you will do fifty push-ups.'

'He was pushed,' Will offered.

'And who might you be?'

'Will Hevenshire, sir.'

'Well Will Hevenshire, nobody asked for your opinion. You will speak when spoken to. Understood?'

'Yes, sir.'

'Good. You will join Thorburn and do fifty push-ups.'

Dane's stomach churned. He felt bad enough being in trouble himself; to have his friend in strife sickened him.

Thankfully, Will walked over, shrugged his shoulders and grinned at Dane with an 'oh well!' look on his face.

'What are you waiting for - trumpets? I said fifty push-ups - NOW! Or shall I make it one hundred?'

Dane and Will dropped to the ground. With a little effort they completed their task. Dane took a step towards his place in line. He felt Will's hand tugging at him and turned around. Seeing the look on Will's face, he stood still.

'Have you finished, Hevenshire?' asked Parnsworth.

'Yes, sir.'

'You may join your colleagues.'

Will walked back to the line.

'Thorburn, have you finished?'

'Yes, sir,' Dane replied.

'Did I tell you to go back to the line?'

'No, sir,' Dane answered, knowing what was coming.

'Yet you were about to do that very thing. You will do another fifty push-ups for acting out of turn.'

Dane's blood started to boil; angry at being in this predicament because of Fenwick, and Parnsworth's apparent glee in making an example of him.

Dropping to the ground once more, he completed another fifty push-ups. His face was flushed by the time he finished. He waited until Parnsworth motioned him to his place in line.

Parnsworth addressed the group.

'The object in leaving you here was to see who could follow orders and who could not. Your instructions were to line up out here – nothing more. It appears some of you were so overawed by the presence of the General that you forgot your orders.'

Dane bristled, knowing that Parnsworth was talking about him.

Parnsworth continued.

'You will do what your superior commands without question. You may not understand the reason behind an order - but it is not your place to question - only to obey. In battle your commander will have more information than you about the issue at hand, and therefore a greater understanding of what is required.

'Your commander's commander will have more information than him, and so on, until it reaches the top – General Silvers, Lord Frederick and King Winston himself. It is therefore absolute – if you are given an order, you will follow it – no questions asked.

'The consequences for disobedience are severe and will not be limited to push-ups.' He paused, glancing at Dane with a look that suggested he'd done him a favour when handing out his punishment.

'In this case, all but two passed. In a battle situation I hope Cadets Thorburn and Hevenshire obey orders better than they did this morning.'

Fenwick let out a suppressed laugh everyone could hear. Parnsworth silenced him with a menacing stare before continuing.

'Training will consist of horsemanship, swordsmanship, archery, agility and fitness, and strategy. You will do two tasks each day. Those remaining after the first phase of training will compete in the Junior Division of the Brindabeare Tournament of Knights.'

Parnsworth paused. There was a general murmuring among the group. The tournament was one of the city's major events; one of the highlights of the year.

'In the past, both General Silvers and I have won the Junior Division. We have also won the Senior Division. I'd expect the winner of the Junior Division to be appointed to the Royal Knights, especially if he was a cadet.

Now retrieve your shields and return immediately.'

The group headed inside, talking among themselves about the Tournament of Knights. Dane relaxed a little, thinking over the possibilities of winning.

Fenwick spoke up so they could all hear.

'No wonder he didn't follow orders - the Princess isn't here to hold his hand!'

Winslow and Harrop laughed.

Dane felt his anger rising, but was reassured when Morgan Hainsley muttered to him, 'Don't worry, we all saw it.' Albert Webster nodded agreement.

Dane grabbed his shield. Like the others it bore the Brindabeare Coat of Arms: a four-pointed cross, with a coloured stone at each point, representing one of the four elements of nature – argent (air), vert (earth), gules (fire) and azure (water); with a gold stone in the middle.

'Thanks for trying to help,' Dane said to Will.

'Don't mention it,' Will replied. 'I told you. You have to watch out for Fenwick.'

'I know. He's had it in for me since we were young.'

'He doesn't like me either. I caught him stealing a colt from our stables. We've avoided each other ever since.'

They made their way outside and joined the others, making sure they lined up away from Fenwick, Winslow and Harrop. Parnsworth appeared, carrying a handful of swords.

'Take a sword and pair off with the person in front or behind you,' he instructed. 'This is an opportunity to assess your ability with sword and shield. You have blunted swords. We want no injuries here.'

Dane was paired with Donovan Braidwood. On Parnsworth's signal he went straight on the attack, landing blow after blow until his opponent fell to the ground. In turn he beat Winslow (who was slow and sloppy) and Hamish Ingham, before finding himself matched against Will.

Will had beaten Albert Webster, Morgan Hainsley and Harrop. Stepping forward to engage, Will nodded to Dane. Dane grinned and nodded back.

'Begin!' yelled Parnsworth.

They circled each other for a few moments, then clashed heavily. Will lunged at Dane's left arm. Dane shot his shield up, deflecting the blow and making a strike of his own in the same movement. Will fended it off.

They faced up again. This time Dane lunged forward with his sword raised, swinging over Will's head. Will blocked the hit and Dane followed with a swipe at his chest. Will stumbled back, raising his shield in the nick of time.

They clashed again. By now the whole group was watching, their current matches finished.

They fought on, searching for a weakness in the other's defense. First Dane's, then Will's shield would let out a loud *clang!* as the opposing sword crashed into it. The battle continued a few minutes before Parnsworth called a halt.

'Enough! We'll call this match a tie.'

Breathing heavily, Dane and Will shook hands and turned to face their next opponents. Will had drawn Henry Featherstone. Dane had drawn Fenwick.

Gathering himself for the fight, Dane caught a glimpse of someone waving at him. Glancing to his left he saw Vanessa and Marilena watching on.

This was his chance. His chance to show Vanessa how good he was going to be - and what better way than to beat Fenwick. Beat him good and make him pay for what happened earlier. Beat him good and make Parnsworth regret doubting his ability. Anger surged through him – Fenwick was going to *feel* some pain.

'Now we'll see who's the better knight around here,' said Fenwick, raising his shield and stepping forward.

'Begin!' yelled Parnsworth.

Dane raised his sword and charged at Fenwick, hitting him with all the strength he could muster. Fenwick staggered trying to absorb the blow, almost falling over. Dane lunged and swung again. Fenwick stumbled, struggling to keep his balance.

This is too easy, Dane thought, moving in for the kill.

In that same instant Harrop stuck his foot out and everything turned upside down. Dane found himself face down on the ground. He rolled over and felt Fenwick's sword on his chest.

'Victory to Cadet Fenwick!' announced Parnsworth.

Fenwick looked at Dane. He had a contemptuous smile on his face, pressing his sword into Dane's chest at the same time.

'I told you we'd find out what a pretender you are,' he sneered.

Dane wrenched the sword away and leapt to his feet.

'You cheating wretch!' he bellowed. 'Sir,' he pleaded, 'surely you saw Harrop trip me over?'

'I saw no such thing,' Parnsworth replied. 'You lost.'

'But sir!'

'I said you lost, Thorburn. You've disobeyed me twice already. Would you like to try for three?'

Seething inside, Dane retrieved his sword and shield. Adding to the anger and injustice he felt, he glanced to where Vanessa and Marilena had been standing and saw them walking away.

Chapter 8

A No-Win Position

The afternoon session gave Dane a chance to demonstrate his ability on horseback. The cadets were given a course to navigate, and he finished so far in front he'd almost finished Thunder's rub-down before Will and a couple of others arrived at the stables.

Will threw his saddle over a rail.

'Tired?' asked Dane.

'I sure am. I haven't had a ride that long in a while. It didn't seem to bother you though.'

'He has a knight-bred horse Hevenshire,' Fenwick spat from the stall opposite. 'It has nothing to do with him. When you're the Princess's little playmate you get all manner of privileges.'

Dane glared at Fenwick, his body red-hot with rage.

'I believe your horse is also knight-bred,' said Morgan.

'Mind your own business,' Fenwick replied, grabbing a bucket and heading for the water trough.

Morgan looked at Dane and Will in turn.

'We have better things to do than worry about him,' he said with a smile.

Dane nodded, letting his anger out with a deep breath before turning his attention back to Thunder.

✦ ✦ ✦

Reflecting on the day's events brought mixed emotions. Dane was grateful he'd made a couple of friends, especially Will, with whom he felt an immediate bond.

At the same time he was annoyed about the incidents with Fenwick. Parnsworth rubbed further salt in those wounds when he re-addressed 'the need to follow orders at all times,' and stressed 'the need for wit as well as skill, ably demonstrated by Cadet Fenwick's defeat of Cadet Thorburn,' before dismissing them for the day.

'I'll get him back,' Dane muttered to Will.

'Don't let it bother to you,' Will replied.

'I can't believe Parnsworth didn't see it. It's like he wants me to fail. What happened to honour and fair play?'

'Fenwick doesn't know what those words mean.'

'I meant Parnsworth!'

'I know!' Will replied laughing. 'Come on, lighten up a little. Like Morgan said, we have better things to do than worry about him.'

'You're right. Tomorrow's another day after all.'

Strategy was the first morning activity. Parnsworth outlined various battle situations and quizzed the cadets on the best strategy to adopt. Everyone struggled trying to answer his questions.

In the latest scenario, Will tried to explain it was best to show military might when shaping up for battle, '- then you could scare an opponent into retreating by the sheer size of your army.'

'And tell me, Hevenshire, how does this defeat the enemy?' asked Parnsworth.

'Well, by the sheer size of our force, they'd see they were out-numbered and retreat.'

'Really? And what if they're able to find others willing to join them and build an army bigger than ours?'

'Well, we'd do the same thing then.'

'I see. But wouldn't there be a point where we'd reach our limits and fight anyway?'

'I guess so,' said Will, becoming more and more uncertain.

'So what has your strategy achieved? Our army is certainly bigger; but now it's more unwieldy, and as a result it's probably *weaker* than it was before.

'In addition, farmers, blacksmiths and the like are now in the army. So who's going to do their jobs and ensure our supplies and weapons are looked after?'

'Well,' Will replied, 'now that you put it like that...'

'I hope I never have to serve under you,' said Parnsworth. 'You've just wiped out the entire city!'

Parnsworth walked to the battle-board. After doubling the size of the Brindabeare Army he released the blocking mechanism. Sure enough, the Brindabeare Army was slow, unwieldy, and quickly defeated.

Will shrank in his seat, humiliated. Dane felt sick for Will and angry with Parnsworth. Why was he so eager to put everyone down? It wasn't enough to point out the mistakes – Parnsworth seemed intent on belittling them in the process.

'What you should do, and indeed what Lord Frederick has advised in the past, is instead of openly demonstrating your might, you *hide* it,' Parnsworth stated, looking Will in the eye.

'Although you may be very strong – you should appear to be weak – very weak. This will encourage your opponent to attack you – on your terms. And when he does, you show your true self, and victory will follow. Even though you *know* what you're doing, give the impression you *don't* know what you're doing – organised chaos I call it. Appear chaotic, while being completely organised.'

The battle-board was re-arranged and the Brindabeare Army was triumphant.

The mid-day meal was a welcome break.

'At this rate I'll be cleaning stables by the end of the week,' Will remarked, lining up with Dane.

'Battle-boards show the most likely result,' said Dane, 'They're not always right – they can't measure courage or the desire to win in unlikely situations.'

Dane thought about some of the lessons he'd had recently. How many of the morning's battles had he been through with Lindstrom? If he'd paid better attention he may have been more help during the session.

His thoughts were interrupted by Fenwick slamming into him. Before he knew it he found himself on the ground, covered in food. Dazed and shaken, it took him a moment to realise what had happened.

Struggling to his feet, he turned to Fenwick, who said loudly, 'Well done Thorburn, now nobody has anything to eat!'

'Why you –' Dane flung himself at Fenwick, knocking him to the ground. Others jumped in to pull them apart, a blur of fists and dirt.

Dane was able to land a couple of punches before Winslow and Harrop grabbed hold of him. Will went to Dane's aid, crashing into them and knocking Harrop out of the way.

Dane wrenched himself free of Winslow's grip and turned on Fenwick again.

'Think you can play me for a fool!' he yelled, landing another blow.

'Argh!' screamed Fenwick. 'Get off! Get off!'

'Not until you own up!' Dane roared.

By now Will, Morgan and the others had managed to subdue Winslow and Harrop, leaving Dane and Fenwick as the only combatants – or, to be true, Dane as the one throwing punches and Fenwick, pinned help-lessly on the ground, wailing for it to stop. To nobody's surprise but his own, with Winslow and Harrop under wraps there didn't seem to be anyone else all that keen to help Fenwick out.

'What is the meaning of this!' boomed Parnsworth, steaming towards them from across the courtyard. 'Thorburn! Release him at once!'

Dane let go of Fenwick and stood up.

'What happened here?' Parnsworth asked Fenwick.

'I was waiting for my meal and Thorburn attacked me sir.'

'You lying —'

'You will not speak until spoken to!' Parnsworth snapped.

Dane fell silent, knowing what was about to happen.

'It was without warning,' said Fenwick. 'He just hit me. He threw me over the table and knocked the food over. He said it was payback for losing at swordfighting yesterday.'

'Sir, it's not true,' said Morgan. Others nodded agreement. 'Ask the cook —'

'I did not ask anyone else to speak! If I want your input I will ask for it! Anything else Fenwick?'

'Nobody had any food except Braidwood sir.'

'I see. So Thorburn, you're such a poor loser you had to seek revenge by carrying out a cowardly, unprovoked attack on a fellow cadet?'

Dane knew whatever he said wouldn't help him. Everyone except Winslow and Harrop was looking on in disbelief, but it made no difference; Parnsworth wasn't going to listen.

'Well? You were keen to interrupt before. You now have the opportunity to speak.'

'I didn't start it sir. Fenwick knocked *me* into the table,' Dane replied. 'But you won't believe it, will you? So punish me and get it over with. I know you want to, and you will - no matter what I say.'

Everyone stood silent, stunned at the outburst.

'What are you waiting for —' Dane said in his best Parnsworth voice, 'Trumpets?'

If it were possible for anyone to show more anger, it would be an achievement. Parnsworth's body quivered with rage. His face contorted, every vein looking as though it might burst.

'You will spend the rest of the day cleaning out the stables,' he said with a slow growl.

'You will not talk to anyone, and you will not rest or eat until every last stable is clean. You will then report to me, to be dismissed only after I have inspected your work. And if I find so much as one strand of hay out of place you will do it again, and then again until I am satisfied. Do I make myself clear?'

'Yes sir!' Dane replied with mock awe.

'Get out of my sight!!'

Dane stomped towards the stables. He didn't bother to look at Fenwick, knowing he'd have a grin a mile wide across his face.

He kicked a bucket in frustration, bouncing it the entire length of one of the stalls.

What hope was there if he couldn't defend himself? Parnsworth hated him, and anytime Fenwick wanted to set him up it looked like he was going to get away with it.

How was he going to be a knight, let alone a Royal Knight if he had to put up with this everyday?

'Dane? What on earth are you doing here?'

Startled out of his thoughts he looked up. Marilena and Vanessa were watching him with puzzled looks on their faces.

'I'm not supposed to talk to anyone.'

'I'm not just anyone,' Vanessa said with a smile, 'or have you forgotten me already?'

'You don't understand,' Dane said in a low voice. 'I have to clean the stables, and I'm not allowed to talk to anyone. I'll only get into more trouble.'

'What do you mean more trouble?' asked Vanessa. 'Why aren't you with the others? We came to see you training, and here you are cleaning out stables. If this is someone's idea of a prank —'

'It's no prank. Fenwick's had it in for me since I started. He's gotten me in trouble three times already. This is the latest task I have to do as punishment.'

'What do you mean he's gotten you into trouble?' asked Marilena.

'Well, this time he slammed into me while we were waiting for our meal, and the food table was knocked over.'

'How could you get into trouble for that?' asked Vanessa.

'I turned around and hit him. I had him pinned on the ground when Parnsworth came out. He only asked Fenwick what happened, and he said I started it.'

'What about the others?' asked Marilena. 'Surely they would have said something?!'

'Like I said, he only asked Fenwick.'

'I'll fix that!' said Vanessa. 'I'll demand a meeting with Parnsworth and make sure he's set straight!'

'You can't do that!' Dane snapped.

'Why not?' she snapped back, shocked that Dane would refuse her help.

'That's exactly why Fenwick hates me. If you go to Parnsworth it'll only make things worse.'

'But this is clearly unfair!'

'Don't you think I know that? Look, the best thing you could do right now is leave me alone and let me finish the stables without getting into more trouble.'

'Fine!' Vanessa yelled, tears welling in her eyes. 'If you don't want my help, or my company, go back and clean the stables then!'

'Vanessa —'

'And you can forget about doing anything on the weekend – I think I might find someone else to spar with!' she said, storming off in a huff.

Dane stared helplessly after her.

'She misses you,' said Marilena, seeing the pained look on her son's face. 'She didn't say it, but it's true. She wanted to see how you were going, and after you were beaten yesterday, we thought you'd enjoy a visit too.'

'I wasn't *beaten*, Mother,' said Dane. 'He cheated. That was Fenwick. One of his cohorts tripped me over.'

Marilena's eyes widened.

'Now you see what I'm dealing with?'

'I do,' Marilena replied. 'But you need to remember that sometimes there are *other* people's feelings to consider in addition to your own. You've now made the Princess feel she's less important to you than horse manure.'

'What? But you know that's not true!'

'*I* am not the one you have to convince,' Marilena replied with a parting smile. She hurried off to catch up with Vanessa.

Things couldn't get any worse. Marilena was right of course. He hadn't given Vanessa a chance to say anything before trying to get rid of her. The last thing he wanted was to get her offside too.

He returned to mucking out of the stables.

'How could I be so stupid,' he cursed, ploughing his broom into a pile of hay and straw.

Chapter 9

An Eagle Is Born

The sun was setting when Dane finished the stables. He looked for Parnsworth and found the barracks deserted. The cadets were doing archery in the main arena. His concern about being seen with Vanessa and Marilena had been for nothing.

He checked the stables twice, not wanting to give Parnsworth reason to find fault with his work. Parnsworth made him wait until the other cadets had stowed their equipment and taken their evening meal before conducting his inspection.

To Dane's relief, Parnsworth was satisfied.

'Pity you aren't as good a knight as you are a stablehand.'

'Yes, sir.'

'You've been in more trouble in two days than I am willing to accept. If you expect to survive, I suggest you do your best to keep out of trouble from now on.'

'Yes, sir.'

'Very well. You may go and join the others.'

Dane made his way to the dining table. Thankfully there was enough food and drink left to enjoy a hearty serving. Cleaning the stables had been hard work.

'And here comes Brindabeare's finest, most incompetent cadet, Dane Thorburn!' announced Fenwick.

Winslow and Harrop laughed.

Dane found his anger rising, overriding his sense of self-control.

'And we all know he's a useless crybaby,' Fenwick went on. 'They say he wet himself the night Raegan tried to kill him.'

Dane snapped. His plate clattered to the floor as he lunged at Fenwick with all his fury. Will, Morgan and Donovan Braidwood stepped between them.

'Forget it,' said Will, while Dane wrestled under his grasp. 'He's not worth it.'

'Don't let him rile you,' added Morgan. 'It's what he wants.'

'I'll get you, Fenwick!' Dane yelled. 'And when I do - you'll wish you were dead!'

Will grabbed hold of Dane and pulled him away.

'Forget it,' Will hissed. 'Just forget it.'

Dane retrieved his plate and helped himself to leftovers.

'How was your afternoon?' asked Will.

'What do you think?' said Dane. 'It was great - cleaning out the stables while everyone else was doing archery.'

'Don't worry. If you can shoot an arrow you didn't miss much.'

Dane gave Will a puzzled look.

'Parnsworth and the officers spent most of the time showing off,' said Morgan. 'Most of us were lucky to get two shots in before we packed up and came back.'

'And how did my friend Fenwick do?'

'Don't worry about him,' said Will. 'He was more likely to shoot himself than the target!'

Dane looked at Will and the others in disbelief.

'It's true,' said Morgan. 'His first shot went so far left it hit the *other* target!'

Smiling for the first time that afternoon, Dane tucked into his meal.

The next morning's activity was another ride. They were to complete a different course this time. Most of it was outside the city, including a ride into the Great Forest. Dane was looking forward to it as a chance to regain his standing among the group.

The cadets gathered outside the Main Gate. Parnsworth's final instructions rang out.

'There are challenges in this activity that were not part of the last,' he announced. 'First, there are four checking points on your map. The watermill, the Great Forest, the North-West Gate, and the barracks. At each checkpoint you are required to retrieve a piece of ribbon. You do not complete the task unless you collect all ribbons.'

A murmur rippled through the group.

'Secondly, at different intervals along the way I have stationed officers. They are instructed to give chase for a short distance in an attempt to catch you.'

Dane felt Thunder shift uneasily next to him.

'Easy, Thunder,' he whispered.

'Should any of you be caught, you are retired from the rest of the event and will take no further part. Is everyone clear?'

There were nods of understanding among the group.

'I said, "Is that clear"?'

'Yes, sir!' the cadets boomed as one.

'Very well. You have your maps. Three.....two.....one.....begin!'

The cadets sprang into their saddles and spurred their mounts toward the river crossing, a cloud of dust trailing behind them. In this task they were to cross the river directly instead of using the bridge.

Dane had ridden this way countless times and knew the shallowest point. Approaching the river he slowed a little and cut sharply to his right, moving away from the rest of the group.

Dane felt himself shift sideways and straightened instinctively in the same movement. He raced on and tried to make sense of it - somehow it felt like his saddle was loose.

They reached the crossing and Dane's move worked. Thunder crossed where the water was barely over his hooves. The others were deeper, where it was heavier going.

Dane emerged first, only to see the first group of officers charging from under the Borsan River Bridge, straight towards him. He urged Thunder on, heading towards the others, hoping to lead the officers straight to them.

The ploy paid off. Dane passed the others and the officers tagged some of them as they exited the river. Henry Featherstone, Hamish Ingham and Winslow were eliminated.

'Good move Dane!' Will yelled, veering to the left and heading towards the first checkpoint.

The watermill was located at one of the fastest running parts of the river. Dane arrived first and headed for the ribbons, tied to a small tree.

He reached down to grab one, and that's when it happened. He felt his whole body move, and with a thud, fell off his mount, saddle and all. Flustered and confused, he stood up and looked in astonishment at his saddle— on the ground with the girth strap undone.

'Well done Thorburn! See you back at barracks!' Fenwick shouted, grabbing a ribbon and riding away.

Thwarted again, Dane screamed in frustration.

'I'll kill you Fenwick!'

Struggling to get the saddle back on, he saw the next group of officers out of the corner of his eye. They were hidden behind the mill, waiting for everyone to arrive before pouncing.

It looked hopeless. There was no time for Dane to get his saddle on before the officers arrived. Fenwick would win again, and there'd be nothing Dane could do to prove he'd been sabotaged.

Now he knew why Thunder had been unsettled before they started, and why he'd felt himself slip sideways - Fenwick had undone the strap while Parnsworth was talking.

The last of the group arrived. The officers were ready to advance.

It was over.

With a surge of adrenaline he reacted.

He threw his saddle to the ground, grabbed a ribbon and jumped on Thunder, bareback. With a quick kick they took flight - better to go down with a fight than a pitiful surrender.

The officers were close before Thunder reached full speed, but once he did, Dane escaped their clutches. He passed Morgan and Donovan Braidwood, who were caught before the officers called off their pursuit.

Dane headed towards the Great Forest Checkpoint. The others were a long way ahead. How long would he last? If he didn't do something he'd be the first one caught.

He needed a plan. How could he survive?

The only way was to avoid them. Go off-course and double back. Make them choose - him or the others. Chase one, or take a chance at four.

It was worth a try.

The others reached the Great Forest and headed straight for the checkpoint - about two miles in, at the four-way junction - a point where the four main tracks intersected. Dane knew the officers would be lurking close by, so he veered to his left, heading towards Reuben's cave.

He was on his own and getting further away from the others with each stride. Once he passed Reuben's cave he turned to the right, in an arc, heading back towards the checkpoint. His plan appeared to be working. He couldn't see anyone in front or behind him.

Approaching the checkpoint he eased Thunder to a walk. He heard the sound of voices through the trees ahead.

'You missed one!' said the first. 'Behind us!'

'Don't be ridiculous Harrop,' answered a second. 'A knight is noble when defeated. Your conduct is quite unbecoming!'

'Let's gather the ribbons and be away,' ordered another.

Dane cursed - he needed a ribbon to complete the task.

He spurred Thunder towards the checkpoint. Racing into the clearing, he saw three officers plus Harrop and Albert Webster. All but Harrop had dismounted.

He knew he had a chance and was on them in a flash. They barely had time to look towards the noise before Thunder charged past and Dane reached out, pulling a ribbon from the hand of one of the officers.

'What the – hey!' yelled the surprised man.

'I told you!' Dane heard Harrop say as he raced away.

He'd done it. One more checkpoint to go – the North-West Gate. This time he needed to be as close to the others as possible. There were no short-cuts or diversions he could use at this checkpoint.

Following the main forest path back towards the city, the only way to catch the others was to head North-East, on a more direct route to the checkpoint. He followed the path until he found a track leading in that direction.

Racing hard up the track, he soon saw a clearing ahead, but when he emerged he wasn't sure where he was.

The main road to Brindabeare was about fifty yards ahead. Will and Fenwick were on this road, behind and below where Dane emerged from the forest. By the time he reached the road they'd overtake him, but he'd regained the distance lost at the watermill.

It took Will a few moments to realise what was happening. On the lookout for officers, he noticed movement ahead to his left. To his surprise a lone rider approached. When he realised who, he flashed a smile.

'Well done Dane!' he yelled.

Dane would have frozen Fenwick's look in time if he could. His reaction was a combination of shock, disbelief and horror. He couldn't believe Dane was still in the game.

Urging Thunder on, Dane joined the main road and caught up to them. None of them spoke on their approach to the checkpoint.

The North-West Gate was not a pleasant place. Its purpose was to alert Brindabeare of any activity within the Highland Mountains, said to be the home of Vrenin, the God of Fire, whose merciless fury destroyed the ancient wizard city of Nadensa at the height of the Great War.

Dane and Will looked at each other and recited the rhyme their mothers had told them when they were very young. 'Do as you're told or you'll suffer the wrath of Vrenin.'

Desolate waste lay between Brindabeare and the mountains; the distance a ride of two to three days.

Finding their ribbons, the riders headed towards the barracks. Moving at a steady pace, they kept their eyes peeled.

There was no resistance until they were less than a mile from barracks, where they were chased by a group of five - a group of five *Royal Knights*. Resplendent in full battle armour, they emerged from their hiding place after a great shout of 'Advance!!!' from none other than General Laramer Silvers himself.

Dane and Will responded immediately, spurring their mounts on and galloping hard up the road. Fenwick was a moment slower to react and he was caught.

Dane and Will raced on, the Royal Knights in lively pursuit.

'Spilt Up!' Dane yelled.

They veered away from one another. Confusing their pursuers for a moment, Dane and Will gained the time needed to make it to barracks before they were caught.

Their arrival was greeted by hearty cheering from the other cadets.

'Well done Dane!' shouted Morgan. 'Well done Will!'

They dismounted and led their horses to the drinking trough, basking in the glory of the moment along the way. Even Hamish Ingham and Henry Featherstone congratulated them. They'd been caught in the first chase, thanks to Dane.

'Great bit of riding!' said Hamish. 'I never would have thought to set a trap like that!'

'Shows real thinking - you scoundrel!' added Henry, shaking Dane's hand.

The revelry continued until everyone arrived. Fenwick was led in by the Royal Knight who'd caught him. Some of the others talked quietly among themselves, smiling at Fenwick's discomfort. He had a look on his face suggesting he'd been sentenced to death.

Parnsworth, with Silvers at his side, called the cadets to order. 'Do the cadets have their ribbons?'

'Yes, sir,' Dane and Will answered together. They stepped forward and handed them over.

'May I speak, Officer Parnsworth?' asked Silvers.

'Of course General.'

Silvers surveyed the group.

'Today I have witnessed an event I would like to share with you all. It appears one of those among you has displayed the very qualities I would expect of a Royal Knight.'

Everyone stood still, hanging on every word.

'It has been brought to my attention that one of the cadets suffered a considerable misfortune during the exercise.'

Dane felt every eye on him.

'But rather than quit, he seized the moment and continued on. He was also clever enough to outsmart the officers at the Great Forest checkpoint and survive the last desperate chase by me and my men with an ingenious tactical decision!'

The vanquished cadets except Fenwick, Winslow and Harrop cheered as one. Dane felt elated and a little embarrassed at the same time.

'It is my hope that by the end of training you will all demonstrate the same qualities!' Silvers concluded.

Climbing into his saddle, he nodded to Parnsworth and rode away, the other Royal Knights following in his wake.

Parnsworth addressed the group.

'Once you tend to your horses the mid-day meal will be served. After yesterday's pathetic effort we will practise archery again this afternoon.'

There was some muttering among the group.

'It was pathetic because nobody had a decent go!' Will hissed.

'You are dismissed – oh, Cadet Thorburn, could I have a word with you please?'

Dane went numb. What now? He followed Parnsworth away from the group.

'Yes, sir?'

'Had the General not been here, I would have disqualified you. It is unacceptable for a knight to lose his saddle. Nothing more than unacceptable incompetence.'

'But sir, it was —'

Parnsworth raised his hand.

'I am not interested. However, as the General said, your efforts during the rest of the activity were commendable. You will now go and retrieve your saddle. Dismissed.'

'Thank you sir.'

Dane headed towards Thunder at the water trough.

He was distraught. In his moment of glory he felt cheated. He'd been praised by the General but Parnsworth had let him know he was still a failure. If the General hadn't been there he probably would have received some sort of punishment for *daring* to succeed.

He untethered Thunder and started to walk towards the Mill Gate.

'Well done Dane!' yelled a couple of cadets.

He waved without looking and kept going. Will made his way over.

'Well that certainly showed 'em, didn't it?' he said, jerking his head in Fenwick's direction.

'Will, I swear, I'm going to kill Fenwick before this is over.'

'But you beat him! For goodness sake, just enjoy it!'

'I was lucky. I could have been caught at the watermill and he would've gotten away with it again!'

'But you weren't caught, were you?' Will nudged him in the ribs. 'I'll save you something for when you get back.'

'Thanks.'

Dane climbed on Thunder and trotted slowly away. As they headed towards the Mill Gate it started to rain. Thunder would be happy. It had been a tough ride, and knight-bred or not, it would have tired him. The rain would cool him down. Dane decided to take his time.

'Let's take the Main Gate instead of the more direct path.' He reached forward, patting Thunder on the neck. 'You did well,' he said softly.

Thunder gave a gentle snort, the rain glistening on his flanks.

Dane let his thoughts wander while he rode. He needed to do something, *anything* to put an end to Fenwick's crusade to destroy him. Today he'd been lucky – it could've been all over before the first ribbon.

Arriving at the watermill, he slid slowly off Thunder and made his way to where he'd left his saddle. To his horror, he saw it wasn't there.

'Just what I need,' he said, kicking the ground in frustration.

'Looking for something Master Dane?'

Dane turned and saw Lord Frederick emerging from the watermill, carrying his saddle in one arm. He breathed a sigh of relief.

'Not a good idea to leave it in the rain,' said Lord Frederick, handing it over.

'Thank you,' Dane replied, slinging it over Thunder and doing up the straps. 'I had no choice. It fell off during the ride.'

Lord Frederick raised an eyebrow.

'Fenwick untied the strap,' Dane answered.

'Are you sure?'

'He's set me up three times already,' said Dane, his anger rising. 'He's out to make sure I fail.'

'And what do you propose to do about it?'

'I'm going to make him pay!' Dane yelled, losing control. 'Winslow and Harrop too!'

Lord Frederick shook his head slowly.

'Anger will not help you,' he replied calmly. 'Nor will needless violence.'

'I've waited my whole life for this and he's trying to get me kicked out! What am I supposed to do? Sit by and do nothing?'

Lord Frederick raised his hand.

'Master Fenwick may want you to falter,' he said in a patient, yet firm tone, 'He may seek to embarrass you and he may take any opportunity he can to belittle you. If you let that affect you and react in the anger of the moment you will most certainly fail. Is that what you want?'

Dane calmed down a little. He could see that Lord Frederick had a point.

'But how do I stop him sabotaging me?'

'Be prepared,' Lord Frederick replied. 'Do not allow him an opportunity. And most of all, do not let him unsettle you - regardless of the provocation. Rise above him - like today. Despite his actions, you rose above him - and you beat him.'

Dane nodded, thinking about the earlier events and seeing them in a new light.

'Look there Master Dane,' said Lord Frederick, pointing towards the Great Forest. 'What do you see?'

'What? The birds? What are they - crows?'

'Yes,' Lord Frederick replied. 'What else?'

'The eagle?' asked Dane, noticing a larger bird circling slightly higher than the others. 'What about it?'

'The eagle is the mightiest of all birds,' Lord Frederick replied with reverence. 'The eagle and the crow want the same food. If the eagle gets it first, the crow will attack it. And when the crow attacks, the eagle soars higher and higher, until it's out of reach.'

Putting it all together, Dane started to understand.

'You're destined for great things Master Dane. But you must remember to soar above your enemies; fly beyond their grasp, and put yourself out of reach.'

Chapter 10

Big Trouble

Dane was a changed young man. Riding back to barracks he felt all the pressure inside him release. A huge weight had lifted off his shoulders.

He'd fallen for Fenwick's trap and become distracted from his real goal - becoming a knight. He was better than that. It would have been easier to let Fenwick have his fun, brush it off and move on. Instead he'd fought fire with fire and ended with ashes.

He laughed at himself. It was time to forget about Fenwick.

When he arrived at the archery session it didn't appear he'd missed anything.

'Move the targets to seventy paces!' barked Parnsworth.

Dane joined the group, lining up with Will.

'What's going on?' he asked.

'They're showing off again.'

'Are we going to learn anything, or are we here to admire the scenery?'

'What?'

'I said —'

'I know what you said,' Will replied. 'It's the first time you've been calm in two days. Maybe that ride back to the watermill did you some good.'

'Great shot Grimshaw!' yelled Parnsworth.

Glancing at the targets, Dane and Will saw that Officer Grimshaw's arrow had almost hit the bullseye.

'Let's see if anyone here is up to that standard. Who will go first? Let's see. Ah yes, Fenwick. Come on lad, step up and show us what you can do.'

Fenwick made his way to the shooting line. Fumbling an arrow out of his quiver, he placed it on his bow, drew back and released. The arrow flew high, sailing over the target and into the butt behind.

Parnsworth was shocked. He'd never seen a cadet shoot so poorly. Fenwick cowered, trembling like a leaf. Laughter rippled down the line of cadets.

'I hope that's not indicative of the rest of you,' said Parnsworth, recovering from what he'd seen.

Relieved he hadn't been belittled further, Fenwick ran to retrieve his stray arrow – anything to get away from that spot.

Morgan and Albert Webster faired better, hitting the edge of the target. Will was next. To everyone's surprise but his own, he sent an arrow whizzing into the target, inches from Grimshaw's.

'Again Hevenshire. Let's see if you can do it again, or whether you were just lucky.'

Will looked at Parnsworth, shrugged his shoulders, and lined up again.

The second shot was even better, landing between the first arrow and the centre. Parnsworth's eyes widened. Several officers applauded. Dane and Morgan cheered. Will shrugged his shoulders and waited for a reaction from Parnsworth. When there was none, he trotted off to retrieve his arrows.

Dane hit the target with his first arrow. Only Will and Donovan Braidwood were better. After everyone had had a turn, Parnsworth ordered the targets moved.

'Seventy paces is too far,' he said. 'A closer target will sharpen your aim. Remember to keep your lead hand steady and your head still.'

The officers moved the targets ten paces closer.

It was Fenwick's turn again. His second shot was better, brushing the top of the target before it hit the butt.

Dane approached Fenwick.

'You're lifting your left arm,' he said. 'And you're rushing your shot. You should slow down a little.'

'Shove off Thorburn,' Fenwick growled. 'What do you care?'

Winslow and Harrop threw menacing stares at him. Dane backed away and joined his place in line.

Will shot a zinger, just left of centre. Parnsworth shook his head in wonder but said nothing. More shouts of delight from the others. Will shrugged and jogged away to retrieve his arrow.

Dane's second shot slammed into the target, close to where Will had hit.

Parnsworth's statement about shooting at a closer target proved to be true. With the exception of Will, who looked likely to hit the bullseye from anywhere, everyone's second arrow was better than their first.

By the end of the session each cadet had fired six arrows. Each improved over the course of the afternoon. Even Fenwick, after an exasperated Parnsworth yelled, 'for goodness sake, keep your arm still!' had some success.

'Did I hear you offering Fenwick advice?' Will asked later that evening.

'Thought it was a shame someone could be that bad,' Dane replied with a smile. 'Didn't take any notice of me though.'

'Where did you learn to fight like that?' Morgan asked the next day.

Dane shrugged. He unbuckled his saddle and threw it over a rail.

'You landed so many blows I felt I was fighting two of you.'

'He's right,' added Will. 'I've never seen someone on horseback fight like you. It was scary.'

Albert Webster rushed over.

'Have you heard?' he asked. 'Hezabar has joined the Candahorn alliance.'

Their mouths dropped open.

'Are you sure?' asked Dane.

'An envoy left the city a little while ago.'

They made their way outside for the mid-day meal. Dane saw some of the others glance towards him and turn away.

'They think it's my fault,' he said.

'That's ridiculous,' said Will.

'No it's not,' said Dane. 'I saw the same looks when word about Candahorn got out.'

They took their meal and joined the others. Albert Webster, Hamish Ingham and Henry Featherstone, who were deep in conversation stopped abruptly when Dane, Will and Morgan sat down.

'What's the matter?' asked Will. 'Are any of you stupid enough to think Dane had something to do with Hezabar joining Candahorn?'

No response. Hamish shifted awkwardly in his seat. Dane saw none of them wanted to look directly at him.

'I said it was crazy,' Albert offered.

'It *is* crazy!' said Morgan. 'He can ride a horse and handle a sword; but how in the name of the gods can that be the cause of a rebellion against Brindabeare?'

Will, Albert and Henry laughed. Dane chuckled and relaxed a little, at the same time noting the reaction from Hamish was a forced smile.

'Very good Princess,' said Lord Frederick. 'One final decision. The regiment you despatched to the North-East is stranded.'

Vanessa considered the situation for a moment.

'Proceed as planned. The greater victory is more important.'

Lord Frederick waved his hands and the battlefield formed in front of them. Lord Frederick's battles contained a greater level of detail than the battle-boards. Among other things the terrain and the weather could be changed, so Vanessa could see the effect of her strategies in different conditions.

The mock battle played out before them. The stranded regiment was lost but the Brindabeare forces were victorious.

'You are aware the regiment was completely wiped out?' said Lord Frederick.

'I had no choice.'

'Very well. Mistress, how do you feel about that?'

Marilena's face was aghast, her mouth trembling.

'Dane was in that regiment! You sent him to his death!'

Vanessa rocked back, horrified.

'What? No! Wait! I've changed my mind! Send half the South Regiment to re-inforce the North-East. We can back-fill to the right to meet the breach in the middle. It would leave a small gap to the west but we'd win *and* save the regiment.'

Vanessa let out a breath.

'I can see the error now. I'm glad it was a rehearsal.'

She glanced at Marilena. Instead of gratitude, Marilena's face was hard and cold.

'What?' Vanessa asked, confused. 'You told me Dane was in trouble and I saved him.'

'What you did,' said Marilena, 'was let your emotions cloud a military decision. Lord Frederick, can you show us the outcome?'

Lord Frederick waved his hands once more.

Vanessa watched the battle unfold. Other regiments were disorganised trying to assist their stranded comrades. The enemy broke through on many fronts; small leaks became raging floods. The Brindabeare army was soundly defeated.

Vanessa looked first at Lord Frederick, then Marilena.

'But,' she said, glowering at Marilena, 'he's your son!'

'No,' said Marilena, 'he's a knight in the Brindabeare Army. You tried to save him and cost Brindabeare the battle. The enemy now rules the land.'

'But —'

'No Princess,' said Lord Frederick. 'Until we informed you of Master Dane's predicament, you were comfortable with your decision. In battle you must displace all emotion and focus on the situation at hand.'

Vanessa nodded.

'How do you think Master Dane would react, knowing the reason behind your actions?'

'He'd never forgive me,' she said without hesitation.

She looked at Marilena with all the hate she could muster. Then she smiled.

'You tricked me.'

Marilena smiled back.

'I know.'

✦ ✦ ✦

The last activity of the week was general fitness and agility. The cadets were to run an obstacle course in pairs.

Paired with Henry Featherstone, Dane eased up towards the end to keep the race close, rather than humiliate his taller and heavier opponent. Will and Fenwick were the fastest pair, with Will overtaking on the rope net for a narrow win.

Parnsworth addressed the group.

'You've completed your first week of training. I'm pleased with what I've seen so far, certain incidents notwithstanding.'

Dane felt Parnsworth's eyes on him.

'Knew he couldn't hold off forever,' he whispered to Will.

'Each week training gets harder, so I suggest you use this time wisely and get plenty of rest. You are to be back by sunrise in three days. Dismissed.'

'What are you going to do over the next two days?' asked Will.

Dane hesitated.

'I'm going to relax and keep out of trouble.'

'Rubbish – you're going to see the Princess and tell her all about your first week's training. When you do, just make sure you get my description right – tall, handsome, dashing –'

Dane grinned, '– bumbling fool,' he added with a friendly jab.

'If you get bored, you can come around to my place – four blocks from the main road on the right, two doors from the farrier.'

'Thanks. See you in three days.'

✦ ✦ ✦

'An update on the Thorburn boy.'

'He does well, My Lord. At riding he excels, and he has considerable ability in the other disciplines. I would say he is Royal Knight material.'

'I see,' Raegan replied. 'We can wait no longer. It is time to act.'

✦ ✦ ✦

Dane was relieved to hear the coded knock.

'I'm glad you came,' he said, checking the hallway.

'Why wouldn't I?' Vanessa replied. 'I've waited all week for this.'

'The other day – at the stables.'

'Forget it,' she smiled. 'It was nothing.' She grabbed Dane by the hand and started running towards Lord Frederick's quarters. 'Come on!'

Excited at her first chance to spar in a week, it didn't take long for Vanessa's enthusiasm to turn to anger and frustration. Dane won several battles in quick succession, and the battered Princess wasn't taking it well.

'Aargh!' she cursed after her latest defeat.

'Sorry,' Dane replied, helping her up. 'I'll take it easier in the next one.'

'No you won't!' she snapped. 'I'm just a bit clumsy.'

'May I offer an observation?' Lord Frederick entered the room. 'Clumsiness is not the problem.'

'What is it then?' asked Vanessa.

'Master Dane's increased ability.'

'What do you mean?' asked Dane.

'You have trained this past week against others equal to or better than you. At present the Princess is no match for you.'

'Oh,' Dane said with a nod. 'Sorry,' he added, looking at Vanessa.

'Don't be silly,' she grinned. 'It'll make me a better fighter. Ready to go again?'

'Not worthy of your presence?' asked Will, stowing his belongings.

'Sorry,' Dane replied. 'I couldn't get away.'

'Don't worry about it. But you can come around anytime you want.'

'Thanks.'

They lined up outside with the others. Parnsworth arrived holding a piece of parchment.

'Before we begin I have an assignment for one of you. Cadet Thorburn, follow me to quarters. The rest of you will wait here.'

Fearing the worst, Dane followed Parnsworth inside.

'Relax,' said Parnsworth, seeing the anxious look on Dane's face. 'A fire has been spotted to the far west of the main road in the Great Forest. I trust you know where that is?'

'Yes, sir.'

'Orders request a scout be sent to investigate. As you are the best rider of the group, you will go.'

'Yes, sir,' said Dane, disappointed he'd miss more training.

'It says this task is to be carried out immediately, by an accomplished rider from the cadet group,' said Parnsworth, reading Dane's mind.

'Yes, sir.'

'Dismissed.'

Heading across the plain towards the Great Forest, Dane looked skyward, searching for a sign of smoke. Clear blue was all he could see; the fire was yet to penetrate the forest canopy.

He'd have to ride right up to it before he found it; if it lay to the far west of the main road it would take all morning to get there.

Soon the novelty of the task wore off and boredom set in. The scenery hadn't changed and Dane found his mind wandering.

It worked exactly as planned. He didn't notice anything until it was too late.

The road swung to the left. Passing an overhanging tree, Dane ducked his head. At that exact moment he was pounced on by a Black Knight. Thunder reared, reacting to the sudden jolt and extra weight, throwing the two of them to the ground.

Dane felt an arm around his neck, choking him. He reached up, gasping for breath. It was no use. He was pinned under the weight of the much larger man, unable to move.

After what seemed an eternity the Black Knight released his grip. Grabbing Dane by the scruff of the neck he stood up, hitting Dane with a couple of heavy punches to the back at the same time.

Dane screamed in agony.

The Black Knight turned him around and hit him in the stomach. Next came a blow across the jaw. Dane staggered and collapsed to the ground.

The boots came next. Two savage kicks to the ribs.

Dane writhed in pain.

He heard the Black Knight walk to his horse, the sound of a sword being unsheathed and knew all hope was lost.

Gasping for breath he turned his head. A short distance away, a pair of steely eyes stared back at him.

Chapter 11
Raegan's Fury

A column of smoke rose from the ground, followed by a loud bang. Through the haze of his blurred vision, Dane saw Raegan step into view.

Raegan walked towards the prone body in front of him. Grabbing Dane by the hair, lifting his head off the ground.

Racked with pain, Dane tried to raise his hands and grab at Raegan's arm.

'You disappoint me Master Thorburn,' Raegan growled, lifting Dane further and further off the ground. 'I thought once you reached the right age there may yet be hope for you. It seems I was wrong. I know you want nothing more than to become a knight, like your father. I shall enjoy ending your life now, so close to your goal.'

Dane felt a rush of anger at mention of his father. With new-found strength he almost wrenched himself free of Raegan's grip. Raegan felt his grip slipping and threw Dane to the ground.

'Still full of honourable intentions. You wish to avenge your father's death? I wonder Jensen, should we allow him the opportunity?'

The Black Knight laughed. 'As you wish My Lord. I will be here, should the need arise.'

Raegan smiled.

'Yes. I'm well informed of Master Thorburn's ability as a swordsman,' he said in mock awe, 'but I doubt your services will be needed.'

He looked at Dane again. 'What do you say? Would you like to strike me down? Avenge your father's death?'

Despite the pain, Dane hauled himself to his feet and stood defiantly in front of Raegan.

'I'll kill you if it's the last thing I do,' he said. Lunging forward, he took a wild, drunken swing at Raegan. He found nothing but air before falling to the ground.

Raegan stared down at Dane.

'Let us hope you have more to offer than that. On your feet.'

Dane looked at Raegan, refusing to move.

'You are in the presence of the Supreme Ruler of Valentaland,' said Raegan, 'and you will show me the proper respect.'

He pointed at Dane with his right hand.

Dane felt an incredible force wrap around his neck. Caught in an invisible, vice-like grip, he was lifted off the ground like a feather and thrown backwards. Slamming into the ground about ten feet away, he nearly blacked out.

'On your feet!' Raegan ordered.

Dane staggered to his feet. He could barely stand, but if he was going to die it would be with honour – he wasn't going to be this wizard's plaything.

Raegan unsheathed his sword and threw it to the ground between them.

Dane stood still.

'The means to killing me lies before you. Pick it up and strike me down.'

Dane's eyes drifted from Raegan to the sword. He knew there'd be no chance of reaching it before Raegan either moved it or killed him.

Dane unsheathed his own sword and threw it away.

'I'm not going to play your game Raegan. Just kill me and get it over with.'

'I see you possess the stubbornness and pigheadedness of your father,' Raegan said with a low growl. 'Know that I took particular pleasure in killing him, given the role he played in having my brother appointed High Governor instead of me. Were it not for him, I would have come to power long ago. Killing you removes the final trace of his futile existence.'

Mustering all his willpower, Dane didn't react. Raegan was baiting him, and no matter what he said, Dane was determined not to bite.

'Tell me, how has it been these last eleven years without your father there to guide you? Not to mention how difficult it must have been for your poor lonely mother. I plan to end her life as well, but I wonder: maybe it would be better to let her experience the combined misery of the deaths of her husband *and* her son?'

Dane snapped. Ignoring the sword he threw himself forward with all his remaining strength, determined to tackle the man in front of him.

Raegan raised his hand, wrapping Dane in the same invisible choker hold he used before. Dane stopped in mid-stride, the force of the grip pressing hard against his throat. He gasped for breath, flailing his arms and legs in vain, trying to free himself.

Raegan held him there, relishing the site of another Thorburn suffering at his hand.

'I grow tired of playing with you,' he said finally. 'However, your death will be slow and painful. I have kept myself busy these past eleven years, perfecting the rarely used but all-powerful Spell of Death. I am able to conjure it in many forms, from the very quick to the painfully slow.'

He walked right up to Dane, maintaining the choker hold, and stood eye-to-eye.

'You shall die slowly. As the fire spreads through your body, you will experience a pain so great you will beg me to end your pathetic life.'

'May Vrenin strike you down Raegan,' Dane said between gulps of air.

Raegan recoiled at hearing the ultimate insult for a Firelord. Before he could react, a bolt of bright light slammed into the ground in front of him. Another landed next to him; another turned a nearby tree to sawdust.

Disoriented for a moment, Raegan released the choker hold. More flashes split the air, slamming into the ground and throwing up huge clouds of dust and debris. Raegan couldn't see more than a couple of feet in any direction.

Jensen panicked.

'My Lord!' he yelled. 'Orders, My Lord!'

Before Raegan could react his body froze. In the next instant a thick web wrapped itself around him, trapping him for the moment.

Streams of light continued to strike, one after the other in rapid succession. Jensen turned this way and that, trying to work out where it was coming from.

Raegan closed his eyes. There was a loud explosion and the web binding him disappeared.

The flashes of light stopped. The air was choked with dust; felled trees and branches were strewn everywhere, the ground pockmarked with holes where the light shafts had struck.

Raegan saw his sword where he'd left it, but Dane was nowhere to be seen. Something in the nearby bushes caught his eye and he strode towards it.

Jensen stepped forward.

'Wh-what happened My Lord?'

Raegan lifted Jensen off the ground with the same choker hold he'd used on Dane. He pointed to the bushes with his other hand.

'You were ordered to find a secure area' he said, pointing to a small hole. 'A scuttler's portal. One of the miserable creatures must have seen what was happening.'

He flung Jensen to the ground.

Coughing and spluttering, Jensen looked up at his master.

'I'm sorry My Lord - I didn't know.'

'Apologies are not acceptable,' said Raegan.

He pointed at Jensen. A bolt of the purest red light shot through the body of the fateful knight. His lifeless body slumped to the ground. A moment later all that remained was an empty suit of black armour.

✦ ✦ ✦

Dane woke with a splitting headache. His whole body was sore. Every bone and muscle ached. Even breathing was an effort. He lifted his head, and it felt as though it might explode.

'Now now Master Dane, lie still,' said a familiar voice somewhere in the haze.

'Where am I?' he asked groggily. 'How did I get here?'

'No need to worry about that now,' the voice replied, 'just lie here and rest.'

'The forest...how did I get out of the forest?'

'No talking Master Dane. Rest, rest.'

Dane rested his head. Everything went dark, and he slept.

✦ ✦ ✦

A fire broke out in the Great Forest, just beyond a large fork in the main road. Serving as a major food source and a barrier between Brindabeare and potential invaders from the West, saving the forest was a high priority.

Initial efforts to contain the fire were unsuccessful. For some reason it kept spreading. Spot-fires were breaking out for no apparent reason.

Lord Frederick found the source of the blaze in a scuttler's cave no one else had seen. Once the burning branch was extinguished, the fire was brought under control.

Causing as much panic as the fire itself was the discovery of a Black Knight's empty armour among the wreckage.

How did it get there?

Was he involved in starting the fire?

Why would he start a fire all the way out here?

How had he been killed?

◆ ◆ ◆

Dane woke once more but didn't feel any better. Voices drifted in and out of the background.

He looked towards the window. Judging by the clear blue sky he guessed he was in one of the castle towers. He looked around the room.

The hospital wing? His was the only bed and there were no nursemaids or patients.

Two figures huddled in the corner. One was small and dressed in rags. The other wore a Masterlord's cape.

'Reuben? Lord Frederick? Where am I?'

Both figures turned around.

'Master Dane!' said Lord Frederick. 'How do you feel?'

Dane sat up and rubbed his head.

'I'm....sore all over. I...don't know what happened. I was in the forest.....A Black Knight.....attacked me....and then I saw.... you.'

He pointed to Reuben.

Reuben nodded. Dane thought he was seeing things. Scuttlers usually go into a hysterical panic if they're forced out of the forest, but Reuben was completely at ease.

'Raegan......Raegan was......going to......kill me.......What happened?'

'Yes Master Dane,' Lord Frederick replied. 'What you say is true. Please, relax a moment and drink.'

Lord Frederick picked up a large goblet from a nearby table. Dane took it uncertainly. Whatever the elixir was it had a horrible smell.

'Drink. It will help to clear your head.'

Dane raised the goblet to his lips, did his best to block out the smell and took a sip. It was warm, and as he swallowed he felt the liquid flow down his throat and somehow branch out inside him, filling his whole body with the warmth he'd tasted.

Looking at Lord Frederick in amazement, he drained the entire contents.

'What is it? It's...incredible.'

'An earth-bound healing remedy. Quite handy whenever I am sick.'

Dane's aches and pains were still there, but he felt a lot better.

'Where are we?' he asked. 'How did I get here?'

'My sleeping quarters,' Lord Frederick replied.

'How did I get here?' he asked again.

'Reuben informed me of your predicament. I was able to divert Raegan's attention long enough to ferry you away.'

'He had me in a spell. He was choking me. I couldn't breathe.'

Lord Frederick nodded.

'A choker hold. Most unpleasant. He was not content just to kill you. He wanted you to suffer terribly.'

Dane nodded, remembering the way it felt tightening around his neck.

'He said something about...the Spell of Death.'

Lord Frederick raised an eyebrow.

'He said he'd – perfected it. How he could kill someone instantly, or make them die slowly.'

Lord Frederick looked at Dane.

'Unfortunately I have no reason to doubt him. Raegan's knowledge of the dark side of the Ruling Elements is unparalleled. Apart from being expressly forbidden, it takes great skill to perform this spell. For those reasons few have dared to try.

'It originates within the darkest side of the Fire Element, and if not done precisely, it enters the body of the person conjuring it, killing them instead. Edan used it to devastating effect during the Great War, and your father was killed by a crude form of the Spell of Death eleven years ago. I am not surprised Raegan has now, as you say "perfected" it.'

'Can you stop it?'

'I am not sure. Without knowing its exact point of origin within the Fire Element it is almost impossible.'

'Then what hope is there? He can use it on anyone he pleases. He could wipe out entire cities.'

'No,' said Lord Frederick with a gentle pat on the shoulder. 'It is not that simple. Conjuring any spell requires energy. Using the Spell of Death in such a way would take more energy than anyone could generate.'

Lord Frederick paced the room.

'It would also disrupt the natural balance of the Ruling Elements, the consequences of which would be dire indeed. It was a similar disruption that led to the destruction of Nadensa during the Great War.'

Dane nodded. He tried to stand but the throbbing in his head made him dizzy. Lord Frederick waved his hand over the goblet and refilled it.

'Have some more.'

Dane drank the elixir, amazed at the effect it continued to have on him.

Lord Frederick spoke gravely.

'This recent activity is cause for concern. It was a matter of time before Raegan emerged. I fear dangerous times are approaching.'

'You will be able to - kill him, won't you?' asked Dane.

'I cannot be certain of that,' said Lord Frederick. 'The fatal wounds in a wizard-bout come from my sword, not my power. To prevail, I need to neutralise Raegan long enough to kill him. At this moment I cannot say whether I will be able to do either when the time comes.'

Dane's jaw dropped, his face aghast. What hope was there if Lord Frederick could not kill Raegan?

Neither spoke for a moment, absorbed in his own thoughts.

They were snapped out of silence by a commotion in the hallway.

'You will let us in this instant!' an angry, determined voice yelled.

'But I have explicit orders!' another protested.

'I don't care!' the first replied. 'Remove yourself immediately!'

Vanessa and Marilena came rushing into the room.

'Lord Frederick!' said Vanessa.

She stopped in her tracks when she saw Reuben and Dane. Dane looked like he'd been beaten by a mob.

'Dane!' she exclaimed, rushing over to him. 'Are you alright? What happened?'

Marilena, already at his side, couldn't believe the sight.

'What in the name of the gods have you been up to?' she said. 'I've been worried half to death!'

'Ladies, please,' said Lord Frederick. 'Master Dane is quite alright.'

'Look at him!' said Marilena. 'He's a mess!'

'Yes, yes,' Lord Frederick nodded, 'but he's quite well. A few more cups of ale and he will be fine.'

'What happened?' Vanessa asked again. 'We saw the fire in the forest, but nobody's seen or heard from you since this morning.'

'Er —' Dane began.

'Princess, Mistress,' said Lord Frederick. 'Master Dane discovered the fire. While there he was attacked by the Black Knight whose armour has since been found. Master Dane gamely confronted him, but was quite overmatched.'

Vanessa and Marilena looked at Dane, stunned. Both mouths gaped; they were at a complete loss for words. Dane said nothing.

'Our loyal friend Reuben witnessed the event and found me in time to assist. I brought Master Dane here, where I could tend to him personally.'

The women seemed frozen to the spot, unable to move or say anything.

'I'm a bit sore, but I'll be fine,' said Dane. 'I probably look worse than I am.'

There was a scream, and everyone turned to Reuben, who was screaming and convulsing madly.

'Manfred!' he said. 'Manfred! He's gone! He's gone!'

Lord Frederick went to the stricken scuttler. With a wave of his hand he lifted Reuben off the ground and placed him on the bed next to Dane. Dane moved out of the way. Reuben continued to convulse, twisting and squirming madly.

Lord Frederick raised his hand again. A short, sharp, azure light shot out, wrapping around Reuben. He stopped struggling and dropped into a deep sleep.

The others watched Lord Frederick gently place his hand on the scuttler's forehead.

'I am afraid there has been a death among the scuttler fraternity,' he said. 'Like all scuttlers, Reuben has the ability to sense when one of his kin has died. His friend Manfred lives near the scene of the fire. He has passed away.'

The others looked mournfully at Reuben. Dane's stomach churned. An innocent life lost in order to save his. The thought sickened him.

'Ladies,' said Lord Frederick, breaking the silence, 'not a word to anyone about what you have seen or heard here.'

They nodded, looked warily at Dane and shuffled out of the room.

'It was Raegan,' Dane said with restrained anger, 'wasn't it?'

'What do you mean?' Lord Frederick replied.

'I know Reuben's friend lived near the scene of the fire,' Dane said in the same angry, determined voice. 'That's how Reuben found me - wasn't it?'

Lord Frederick nodded.

'And Raegan killed him - didn't he?'

Lord Frederick made no reply.

'In doing a good turn to save me, Reuben's friend is dead.' Dane's anger continued to rise.

'You must not blame yourself,' Lord Frederick said gently.

'But an innocent scuttler is dead!' Dane yelled. He threw his goblet against the wall, smashing it to pieces.

'Master Dane,' said Lord Frederick, waving his hand and restoring the shattered goblet, 'you must understand that fate can bring unfortunate consequences. Innocent lives are often lost in the battle of good and evil. The loss of any life, good *or* bad is regrettable, but we must accept what has happened and move on. You will do yourself no good feeling guilty about events beyond your control.'

He refilled the goblet and handed it back. Dane took it, hesitated for a moment and started to drink. It seemed to calm him as he felt the warmth and healing powers of the elixir coursing through his body.

'I will kill Raegan if it's the last thing I do,' he said with grim determination. 'If it's the last thing I do.'

Chapter 12

Tension Mounts

Dane had become some kind of hero. News of his encounter spread throughout the land. Everyone had a different version of the story to tell.

'.....and he killed the Black Knight all by himself!'

'I heard there was a group of them who lit the fire, and he chased them until he caught one!'

'...and by the time Lord Frederick got there it was all over!'

When he arrived back at quarters, all but three cadets wanted to hear the story firsthand.

'Come on,' Morgan goaded, 'you beat a Black Knight - *by yourself!*'

'I don't want to talk about it,' Dane replied, escaping to the stables.

As always, Thunder was glad to see him, nuzzling against him while Dane gave him a gentle pat.

'I'm glad you're alright,' said Dane, checking him all over. 'We had a bit of a scare.'

Hamish Ingham walked over with a feed bucket, offering it to Thunder.

'I'm sorry I doubted you,' he said. 'I let silly ideas into my head. All that talk about Candahorn and all.'

Dane nodded.

'Some people said you were in league with the Black Knights,' said Hamish. 'I can't believe I thought it might be true.'

'Don't worry about it,' said Dane.

Relieved, Hamish smiled and went back to the feeding trough.

Will came in and sidled over.

'How are you doing?'

'I'm a bit sore, but I'll survive,' said Dane.

'A Black Knight,' Will said in a low voice. 'It would have scared the hell out of me. It's lucky you got out alive.'

'I know. But everyone thinks I'm a hero. The truth would disappoint them.'

Will looked at him, waiting for him to go on.

'Not that I can say anything. I'm sworn to secrecy.'

Will let out a low whistle.

'You must've seen something really bad. Was it – Raegan?'

Dane dropped the grooming brush and it thumped onto the floor. He picked it up and stood there for a moment, not knowing what to say or do.

They looked at each other, and without saying anything, an understanding was reached. Will's eyes widened. Dane nodded and continued to groom Thunder. Will tended to his horse before he and Dane grabbed their shields and headed to the morning's swordfighting session.

At the mid-day meal Fenwick turned the topic back to the day before.

'I heard you fell over yourself and screamed so loud Lord Frederick heard you from the castle.'

Dane said nothing. He was determined not to buy in to Fenwick's game.

'Nothing to say?' Fenwick taunted. 'I must be right then.'

Gritting his teeth, but still in control of himself, Dane didn't answer.

'Just as I thought,' Fenwick continued. 'Nothing but a hopeless cry-baby. The city may think you're a hero, but we know what really happened, don't we?'

Dane stood up, turning to face Fenwick, who sprang to his feet, ready for the assault. Winslow and Harrop moved in behind him. Seeing what was about to unfold, Will and Morgan dropped their plates and went to Dane's aid.

Will grabbed Dane by the shoulders and Morgan whispered in his ear. Dane nodded and waited while Morgan raced off. He returned, holding a large, thick plank of wood. Standing between the combatants, he held the plank in front of Fenwick.

'If you provoke Dane again, this is what he'll do,' he said, turning to hold the plank in front of Dane, gripping the ends tightly.

Dane faced up to Morgan, focusing his energy, gathering his strength.

With a sudden surge, he hit the plank in the middle with his fist, smashing it to pieces. Fenwick recoiled. Everyone else went wide-eyed and gasped. Winslow and Harrop shrunk back.

'So I wouldn't get him mad if I were you!' said Morgan, shaking his finger at Fenwick as a mother would at a naughty child.

Fenwick and his posse stormed off. The rest of the cadets laughed.

'Nice one,' said Dane, shaking Morgan's hand.

'Anytime,' Morgan replied with a grin. 'I'll throw the pieces away before they get the chance to see the hoof prints in them.'

Parnsworth was his usual self in the afternoon strategy session. Nothing the cadets came up with was good enough, and he let them know in no uncertain terms.

'We're now on an increased war footing, yet you know nothing about the most basic strategy! How can you expect to survive if you don't know the plan?'

'Sir?' asked Will.

'Yes Hevenshire?'

'If we follow orders, why does it matter? You said it yourself. We have to obey orders without question. So why should we have to know all this?'

'Hevenshire, I don't know what I'm going to do with you,' Parnsworth replied. 'One day it may be you who issues the orders. And how can you do that if you don't understand the strategy - the reason behind a course of action?

'It was exactly that attitude that almost led to a defeat in the Pardosta uprising against Grelfan some twenty years ago. The 3rd Battalion was supposed to defend a river crossing at all costs. It was a trap to draw the enemy forward in a false sense of victory. But when the 2nd Battalion appeared to falter, they went to assist, instead of staying where they were.'

He strode among the cadets, lecturing them like some all-knowing-all-conquering war hero. He went on.

'The General thought he was doing the right thing, but as a result they were outflanked by enemy forces and almost wiped out. If he'd understood the strategy, they would have been safe.'

He continued prancing among the group.

'To draw the enemy into the trap, the 2nd Battalion had to appear to collapse; otherwise the plan wouldn't work.'

He came to stand in front of Will, and rammed the last point home, bending down to look Will eye-to-eye.

'Yet the battle was almost lost, and it was purely because the General – a senior commander - didn't understand the strategy! Let that be a lesson to all of you!'

Will dropped his head. Dane looked at Parnsworth with anger in his eyes. Why did he have to make his point in a way that made them look like fools?

'I think he does it for fun,' Morgan reflected at dinner.

Dane and Will nodded.

'But you know what they say?' asked Morgan.

'No,' Dane replied. 'What do they say?'

'Those that can, lead armies,' said Morgan in his best Parnsworth voice, 'and those that can't, lead cadets.'

The whole group laughed.

◆ ◆ ◆

'I am about to become the ruler of Brindabeare,' he snarls. 'And there is no place for you in my kingdom'...

A flash of red – his father falls to the floor...

'Father!...Father!...Come back!...Come back!'

He kicks.

He screams...

...he charges.

A flash of light and the swing of a blade.

Raegan falls...

Dane woke in a cold sweat. He noticed the ache in his chin - another nightmare.

Or was it?

A flash of light and the swing of a blade.

What was that?

He looked around. The other cadets were sound asleep. It was pitch black outside. He rolled over and went back to sleep.

Raegan falls...

Raegan falls...

◆ ◆ ◆

They were woken early the next morning by the sound of trumpets. Dane shot up out of bed. He'd never heard trumpets like this before.

He looked at the others.

'What's going on?' he asked Will.

Will shrugged.

'No idea.'

Parnsworth came striding into the room.

'Everyone up! I want you dressed and outside immediately!'

The cadets obeyed, struggling to get tired limbs into clothes and outside into the cold, early morning air.

'The trumpets you hear are battle trumpets,' said Parnsworth.

Eyes widened.

'The entire army is being summoned to form up and wait for instructions. There is a need for the cadet quarters to be used, and with so little training behind you, General Silvers does not deem your presence necessary. You are to clear your things and assemble again tomorrow. Dismissed.'

He turned on his heel and left.

Everyone stood looking at each other.

A war? A war! Brindabeare was going to war!

Heading inside to pack their belongings, Dane and Will mulled over the possibilities.

'Who could it be?' asked Will. 'It must be Candahorn.'

'Maybe,' Dane replied.

'Who else could it be?'

'They may have one of the provinces start something. I doubt they'd declare war on us as their first move. I think they would flex their muscles in the provinces first.'

'You may be right,' said Will, thinking it over.

'Thorburn!' yelled Parnsworth. 'Stop dawdling and get your belongings out of here now!'

'Yes sir,' said Dane through gritted teeth.

'You too Hevenshire!'

'Sir, who's attacking us?' asked Dane.

'That is not you concern!' Parnsworth thundered. 'You're only concern is to empty these quarters of your things, and you will do it now!'

He turned and stormed off, barking instructions at the others as he went.

By the time the morning sun appeared Dane was searching the castle for news about what was happening.

People rushed around, speaking in hushed tones, serious looks on their faces. Where he'd almost been a celebrity the day before, now he couldn't get a word in edgeways with anyone.

He knew he wouldn't find Lord Frederick or the other members of the Council; they would be meeting with the King, General Silvers and Regiment Commanders to plan the battle. There were others he could tap for information - people like Laidlaw, the Clerk of the Court, who knew anything and everything that went on in and around the castle. This time all he got was an abrupt, 'too busy.'

He stalked around like a caged lion, going from one place to the other, unable to glean anything about what was to come.

At one point he found himself, of all places, in the South Tower, looking out the schoolroom window. He scanned the horizon, straining to see any trace of oncoming trouble. Nothing. Not even a hint of smoke or dust to indicate an enemy approach. Where could they be? Who were they?

'Dane?'

Turning away from the window, he saw Vanessa walking towards him with a puzzled look on her face.

'What are you doing here?'

'Trying to catch up on my study.'

Vanessa smiled.

'I was looking to see if there was a sign of an enemy approach.'

'Well, no need to worry about that. There is no —' She caught herself and stopped in mid-sentence.

'There is no what?' asked Dane.

Vanessa hesitated.

'I – I can't say.'

'Why not?' Dane demanded. 'Are we going to be invaded or not?'

'I'm - not allowed to say - Council orders.'

'Vanessa, it's me!' Dane pleaded. 'And we're in here - who's going to know?'

Vanessa hesitated but said nothing. Dane felt his anger starting to boil up inside him. 'Very well,' said Vanessa, after an uneasy silence. 'I'll tell you on one condition.'

'Agreed,' Dane replied without thinking. 'Name your price.'

'I want to know the truth about what happened in the forest.'

Dane was floored. He felt like he'd been hit in the stomach. What was he going to do now? He'd promised Lord Frederick he wouldn't tell anyone.

He looked at Vanessa, who had a wry smile on her face. She knew that he knew he was trapped, and she felt good about it. She couldn't lose. She'd either hear what she wanted to hear, or she'd say nothing.

Defeated, Dane smiled in spite of himself.

'You're good you know.'

'I know,' Vanessa replied. 'If you learned to think before acting you wouldn't have been caught out so easily. What's it going to be?'

'You win,' Dane conceded. 'But if Lord Frederick finds out he'll never trust me again. I'll be ruined. I won't be able to show myself in the castle.'

Vanessa smiled.

'I'll be an outcast. I'll have to go and live with Reuben - no, his cave's too small. Maybe I'll find a rock somewhere.'

'All right!' Vanessa said laughing. 'I won't tell! Are we going to do this or not?'

'What's wrong with what you were told?' asked Dane.

'Almost all of it.'

'Like what?'

'Well, let's start with this. If you came across a Black Knight, why did it end up in a fight? Why didn't you come back and tell someone? I know you wouldn't have been silly enough to challenge him.'

Dane nodded.

'You're right. I didn't find him - he found me. He jumped out of a tree. He was planted there, waiting for me to ride past.'

'That means someone in Brindabeare set you up,' said Vanessa, startled at the realisation.

'I know. But who? The only person I can think of is Parnsworth.'

'Impossible. Parnsworth served under your father when he was a Commander. He'd never do it.'

Dane's jaw dropped.

'What!?'

'Yes. As much as you think he hates you, he loved your father.'

'Well I'll be,' said Dane, shaking his head. 'Very well. I've told you what you want to know. Now it's your turn.'

'No you haven't,' Vanessa replied. 'There's more.'

More questions were fired at him, and soon Vanessa knew everything. She was nervous, but at the same time angry and defiant. She seemed to take it as a personal affront that Raegan was actively creating trouble.

In her demeanor, Dane saw many of the same subtle reactions and expressions of her father. She was cool, calm, calculating, and didn't give much away. For the first time Dane realised he was talking to the next ruler of Valentaland.

'So who's about to invade us?'

Vanessa laughed.

'Nobody's invading us.'

'What!!?' Dane said with wide eyes. 'The trumpets – Parnsworth said they were battle trumpets. We had to empty quarters.'

'Battle trumpets don't always mean we're about to be invaded. It means the entire army is activated.'

'What's happening then?'

'Pardosta. We've received word they're planning to invade Grelfan.'

'Why? Grelfan is peaceful. They've never attacked anyone.'

'We know. But Pardosta has attacked them in the past. In one battle they nearly beat us.'

Dane nodded, harking back to the previous day's strategy lesson. Grelfan was located between the Astuvius River and the Great Forest, the nearest province to Brindabeare in the lower South-West. Pardosta, their nearest neighbour, was on the other side of the river.

'What are we going to do?'

'We're sending two battalions. They leave tonight, and they'll reach Grelfan in a couple of days. Pardosta won't be in a position to do anything before then.'

Dane thought for a moment.

'It's starting, isn't it?' he said, as much to himself as to Vanessa.

Vanessa gave him a puzzled look.

'What?'

'Battles. Wars. Skirmishes. Call it what you want. It's going to start all over again. Raegan wants to rule Valentaland, and what better way to do it than to get Candahorn and her allies to rise up against us. They're using this first battle as a test.'

Vanessa nodded.

'It was one of the things we discussed at Council. Times have changed. We knew peace wouldn't last forever, at least not as it has for the last ten years, but we didn't expect to have to move to a full war footing so soon. It seems to have fallen apart in no time at all. We can only hope the rest of our spy network is as good at warning us in advance as Cromfeld and his team in Pardosta.'

Chapter 13

Not Just A Cadet

Cromfeld couldn't move. His hands and feet were bound; he was blindfolded and a gag was in his mouth.

'Remove the binds,' a voice ordered somewhere in front of him.

Rough hands untied him, tore off the blindfold and removed the gag. Reflexes took over and several things happened at once. He was momentarily blinded by the light in the room, he rubbed his hands instinctively, then retched on the floor.

Gathering his bearings, he looked around. The room was empty, except for a couple of large chairs at the end, behind which a large curtain hung.

Straining his eyes, he looked harder. When he saw the Black Knights he started to understand. They stood guard over someone who looked like Lord Frederick.

'Who are you?' he said with a strained, dry voice.

'I am Lord Raegan,' the other replied. 'And I am disappointed in you Cromfeld. You may know little about me, but I know everything about you. And what I know displeases me.'

Cromfeld looked around him.

'W-what do you mean?' he stammered.

Raegan stood and walked forward a couple of paces.

'I know you are a stablehand; but you are also a spy – a Brindabeare spy.'

'I – I – d-don't know what you mean,' Cromfeld replied.

'You are a spy and a traitor.'

'Please,' Cromfeld begged, 'there must be some mistake. I'm no spy. I don't know what you're talking about.'

Raegan clicked his fingers and two Black Knights disappeared behind the curtain. They were back in moments, dragging a young boy and a woman. They were bound and gagged, just as Cromfeld had been.

Cromfeld looked at them in horror. They were wide-eyed with fear.

Rushing towards them he stopped in mid-stride, an invisible, vice-like grip wrapped around his throat. He struggled, gasping at the air around him to try and free himself.

Raegan flicked his hand towards the back wall. Cromfeld flew through the air, landing heavily several feet away. He hit the floor with a thud, the force almost knocking him out. He struggled weakly to his feet.

'We will try again,' said Raegan. 'You will confess your crimes against Pardosta, or I will end the lives of your wife and child. I will not ask again.'

Cromfeld glanced towards them. His wife looked as though she was about to faint; his son was scared beyond his wits. They looked at him pleadingly, desperately, hoping he could get them away from here.

He turned back to Raegan.

'It's true,' he said.

Raegan nodded.

Stepping down from the rostrum, he walked forward. Cromfeld recoiled in fear.

'There is no need to worry,' said Raegan. 'Promise you will never betray Pardosta again and all shall be forgiven.'

Cromfeld looked at Raegan, unsure what do.

'Swear you will never spy for Brindabeare again, and you and your family can go free.'

Cromfeld looked despairingly at them. He knew it wasn't going to be that simple, but seeing the pleading looks on their faces, he did as he was told.

'I swear I will never spy for Brindabeare again,' he said.

Raegan smiled.

'No,' he replied in a cold, hard voice that chilled Cromfeld to the core of his being, 'you won't.'

A shot of bright red light hit the boy Cromfeld in the chest. For an instant nothing happened, then suddenly his body started to smoke from head to toe. A sizzling sound grew louder as the force of the fire passing through the little body grew in intensity.

He started to shake, then let out a final, muffled scream, before slumping to the floor.

The boy's mother collapsed. Cromfeld rushed forward. Raegan stopped him with a choker-hold. Cromfeld's eyes bulged as the grip tightened.

'You see, Cromfeld,' said Raegan in the same cold, hard voice, 'you have disrupted my plans, and your traitorous acts will lead to the loss of Pardostan lives. Anyone who crosses me pays a very high price. In your case, it will be the lives of those most dear.'

Cromfeld struggled under the grip, trying to free himself and rush at Raegan at the same time.

'I chose the boy first, so your wife would see the consequences of your actions.'

He released the choker-hold, flicked his hand, and Cromfeld's wife flew through the air, landing on the floor in front of them. Cromfeld was seized by a Black Knight before he had time to react.

Raegan lifted Cromfeld's wife off the floor and snapped his fingers. She stared in shock at her predicament; suspended off the floor, looking directly into the face of the man who killed her son.

'Hello my dear,' said Raegan. 'I thought I would wake you, so you could offer your goodbyes before I killed you.'

She looked at Cromfeld, struggling desperately under the grip of the Black Knight.

'Rebecca!' cried Cromfeld, grappling with the strong hands around him, 'I'm sorry! I'm sorry!'

'Dearest Rebecca,' said Raegan, 'it is my duty to inform you your husband is guilty of treason. An offence of this magnitude exacts the most severe punishment. Your son is already dead, and you are about to suffer the same fate...' He trailed off, thinking.

Cromfeld kicked and struggled, almost breaking free in his desperation to save his wife.

'However,' said Raegan, recovering his thoughts, 'I have another idea. I have decided to let you live.'

He flicked his hand. Rebecca fell to the floor.

'But he will die.'

Another shot of red left his hand, hitting Cromfeld in the chest. This time it had far greater force. In an instant Cromfeld's body went limp, slumping to the floor.

Raegan pointed to Rebecca, and the rope and gag were removed. He bent down and picked her up roughly by the hair. 'You will go to Brindabeare. You will find Lord Frederick and the King, and you will tell them exactly what transpired here. You will tell them if they continue to interfere with my plans, more innocent lives will be lost.'

There was no battle at Grelfan. Once they'd been found out, Pardosta didn't mobilise their army. Brindabeare sent two battalions to the area as a show of force and a message they were ready and able to defend the peace they'd maintained for the last three hundred years.

Rebecca was taken in and looked after. While careful not to ignore the enormity of what had happened to her, news of her ordeal stayed under wraps.

The feeling of unease and approaching hostilities continued. People were more guarded and cautious in their daily lives, the care-free air of lasting peace replaced by an upswell of simmering tension.

Cadet training became more intense, some sessions stretching into the evening before they were dismissed for the day.

No one could match Dane on horseback, and when it came to mounted swordfighting he was unbeatable.

In the same vein, Will was a natural archer. Any distance, rapid fire or a deliberate set shot, you could wager he'd hit close to the bullseye every time.

At the opposite end of the scale, watching Fenwick with a bow and arrow was painful in the extreme. Whenever he lined up there were no guarantees he'd hit the target. Dane happily watched him suffer after the response he'd received when trying to offer advice.

At swordfighting, Dane, Will and Fenwick were the best of the group. Each won as many as they lost against each other, some battles going on for an age before they were stopped. In response to this Parnsworth started matching them against Junior Officers.

Agility was a similar story. They had to be pitted against each other or they'd win easily. To ensure a fair race, Parnsworth would pit the unmatched cadet against Officer Eagleton, a Junior Officer who excelled at this activity.

Strategy sessions continued. As tedious as they were, Dane started to see the benefit. There was no use having the raw ability to fight if you didn't have some idea of the overall plan.

You needed to know when to advance and when to retreat; how to ensure you weren't outmaneuvered, how to anticipate the enemy's moves, and how to react in the heat of battle if things change from the original plan. He could even see the benefit of knowing and observing Brindabeare's military protocols.

Parnsworth continued to make the sessions painful.

'I've never had such a poor group,' he'd say again and again. 'I hope I'm never in command of you in battle.'

'So do we,' Dane would whisper to Will, the joke relieving the tension for a moment.

Dane felt a surge of pride whenever his father was mentioned for his role in formulating the strategy of past battles. At the same time he wondered whether his father had had to suffer through sessions like these when he was a cadet.

Lord Frederick and Raegan also figured prominently in preparing battle plans. Dane tried to address the ramifications of a battle against Raegan, only to have it dismissed out of hand.

'Surely he'd know our weaknesses and be able to exploit them,' he offered.

'Don't be ridiculous Thorburn,' Parnsworth snapped. 'Wizard or not, he wouldn't stand a chance against the Brindabeare Army.'

Fenwick continued his crusade to make life miserable for Dane, and by association, Will as well. Dane and Will did their best to avoid direct confrontations and had some willing helpers.

Winslow made the mistake of approaching Morgan at one point, seeking his assistance in carrying out one of their schemes, to which Morgan replied at the top of his voice, 'So, you want me to help *you, Fenwick, and Harrop* hide Dane's equipment, do you?'

All eyes turned to Morgan. Seizing the moment he slapped his hand to his face, reeled back in horror, and added, 'but - wouldn't that be - I don't know - like - *stealing?*'

All but the guilty roared with laughter, with Morgan adding several dramatic gestures of shocked outrage and, 'How could you's?' before Winslow slunk away. Fenwick could do nothing but suffer the public humiliation of his plan backfiring.

✦ ✦ ✦

Vanessa made sure her weekend sparring with Dane continued, and she insisted he go all out in their battles.

'I don't want you taking it easy,' she said. 'I may need to defend myself one day. I need to be able to fight for my life.'

'If you want that kind of training, you need a Royal Knight to spar with you,' Dane replied. 'They're better than me.'

'You know that can't happen,' she said with a wry grin.

'All the same, I'm just a cadet.'

'That may be, but you have real talent.'

'What do you mean?'

'Like the other day, down at the river.'

'You saw that?' asked Dane.

'I wasn't really paying attention. Lord Frederick and father were talking, and sort of watching all of you – and suddenly General Silvers said, "Who is that?" We saw you beat two knights and make it across the river or something.

'That was the point of the exercise. It was no big deal.'

'It *was* a big deal,' Vanessa countered. 'Lord Frederick and father were amazed you did it. Silvers was speechless. He said he'd never seen *anyone* cross the river. Parnsworth deliberately sets that exercise up so everyone fails - but you *beat* them. Father laughed. He was sure Parnsworth wouldn't be happy you'd outwitted him.'

'He was right!' said Dane with a grin. 'He was on me the rest of the day.'

'The point is, you weren't supposed to do it, but you did. That takes special talent - something no other person could do until you did it.'

Dane smiled.

'So,' said Vanessa with a friendly jab, 'you're not "just a cadet". Same time tomorrow?'

✦ ✦ ✦

Parnsworth changed the mounted swordfighting task the following week.

In addition to getting past the two Royal Knights at the river, if they made it that far they had to proceed up the hill, past another Royal Knight and capture the 'castle'.

It seemed an impossible task - none of the cadets who'd tried had made it out of the water.

Dane prepared for his turn. Focused on the task he didn't hear any of the words of encouragement from the others. He studied the course ahead of him – Somerville and Chamberlain, the two Royal Knights at the other side of the river; Simplot, the other knight, halfway up the hill, and the 'castle' – his target – which he noticed contained Parnsworth, the King, Lord Frederick, Silvers, Vanessa, Marilena, and Salsbury.

He checked everything one last time, saddled up and raised his sword. Parnsworth nodded, a trumpet sounded, and Dane sent Thunder charging towards the river.

He made it about a third of the way before being met by the Royal Knights; water spraying everywhere as the two forces collided.

Noting the outcome of the earlier battles, Dane took a different approach to the other cadets, veering to his right a few strides before contact and turning sharply to the left in the next instant. This meant he was attacking from the enemy's left flank instead of front-on.

'Rather unorthodox,' Silvers noted from his vantage point.

'If he has the strength to survive, I would say rather ingenious,' said Lord Frederick. 'He now has only one flank to defend. The only way the others can escape is if *they* are able to get past *him.*'

Before the Royal Knights had time to realise their mistake, Thunder charged into the front flanks of Somerville's horse. The confused rider was forced to turn abruptly to his right. In the same instant, Dane swung across his body, unseating the hapless knight before he knew what happened.

Dane kept Thunder surging forward, and the stunned second knight, in a worse position than his partner, raised his sword in the nick of time. Now it was a one-on-one battle, and Dane had all the advantages.

He kept Thunder boring in on the knight's left, making sure if any ground was to be given, it would be on his terms. Chamberlain tried valiantly, but it was a lost cause and not long before the second Royal Knight hit the water with a splash.

Gathering himself, Dane turned Thunder to his right, heading for the other side of the river. He'd made it this far, but the odds were still against him. He had to get out of the water and get Thunder moving as quickly as possible before he met Simplot, who was now charging downhill towards him.

'He's caught between the bridge and the enemy,' Silvers noted. 'Now he's the one with no way out.'

Dane barely made it out when his assailant confronted him. The *clang!* of sword on sword rang out. Dane managed to deflect the first blow.

Gathering his thoughts quickly, he didn't try to fight back straight away. He figured his best chance of success was to absorb what Simplot was throwing at him and wait for a later opportunity. The longer it went on, the better his chances.

After deflecting the initial blows he was able to hold his ground. Dane could see the frustration on the face of his opponent. Simplot expected a quick kill and every blow that wasn't bothered him.

Dane made his move. Using the momentum of his opponent to advantage, he let Thunder move back towards the river. Sensing a retreat, Simplot swung at him with renewed vigour.

'I think he's finally tiring,' said Silvers.

Dane eased back, moving in time with the downward force of each swing of Simplot's sword. Soon Thunder's hindquarters were splashing in the water. Sensing the end was near, Simplot swung harder still.

Dane deflected blow after blow, concentrating with every ounce of energy.

Thunder had all his legs in the water now, Simplot was jubilant – another moment and...

In a flash it happened.

The other horse reached the water and hesitated - the combined result of downward force and the unsteadiness of the first step on new ground.

At that exact moment, Simplot had his sword at the top of its arc, ready to deliver another blow. Dane had worked it precisely, and in the instant all this happened he reached across to the other horse, grabbing its bridle and pulled down on it with all his strength.

The horse stumbled, throwing Simplot forward in the same motion and upsetting the timing of the blow he was about to make. Dane swung his shield across his body, clubbing Simplot and knocking him out of the saddle.

With a giant splash the third Royal Knight hit the water.

At first nothing happened. It took a moment for the onlookers to realise what they'd seen.

Dane was exiting the water... he hadn't been beaten...in fact he'd... won.

Then the commotion broke out. Loud whoops and cheers from the other side of the river. With three obvious exceptions the cadets were going crazy with delight. Will was on the bridge shouting, 'Unbelievable! Unbelievable! Un-be-lieveable!'

There was applause from the 'castle'. The vanquished Royal Knights shook Dane's hand.

For a few moments he didn't move. He didn't appear to be in the present. He didn't seem to realise what he'd done or where he was. A slap from Will jolted him back to reality.

'Amazing!' Will boomed. 'I've never seen anything like it!'

'Thanks,' Dane offered in reply.

'Get up there and take the castle!'

Looking up, Dane saw Vanessa and Marilena smiling and waving. With Thunder at a walk, he headed towards them. The King, Lord Frederick and Silvers looked on in stunned amazement.

He dismounted and looked directly at Parnsworth, daring him to find fault with what he'd done. Parnsworth met the challenge with an approving nod.

Dane glanced at Vanessa and Marilena. Without saying a word they understood – they'd save their congratulations for later.

When everyone had gathered at the 'castle' the King made a short speech.

'I have never seen anything like what I have seen today. Master Thorburn it is my privilege to know you will soon be a member of my army.'

Dane bowed. 'Thank you, Sire,' he said, and almost all present applauded.

'Sommerville, Chamberlain, Simplot, tend to Thorburn's horse and equipment.'

The three Royal Knights moved forward. They shook hands with Dane again, took Thunder, his sword and shield, and helped remove his armour before heading towards the cadet quarters.

'Officer Parnsworth,' said the King with a wry grin, 'you may have to further revise your strategy. I believe this is the second time Master Thorburn has outsmarted you.'

'I don't think there's a problem with the strategy, Sire,' Parnsworth replied. 'The problem is that Master Thorburn may have some of his father in him after all.'

Chapter 14
The Tournament of Knights

With the first part of training over, there would be a short break while the city absorbed itself in the Tournament of Knights.

It also meant that for the first time in three months Dane and Vanessa were able to have an afternoon ride together.

'I've missed this,' said Vanessa, glancing towards the forest. Buttons was eager to race too, jerking her head from side to side and shifting restlessly on the spot.

'Me too,' nodded Dane.

On their first run to the forest clearing, Dane saw an image out of the corner of his eye. He stopped Thunder in his tracks and looked around.

Nothing.

He headed into the forest.

There! – to his left.

It's gone – disappeared – just like before.

He looked around, his heart racing. Where was it? He listened – maybe the sound would lead him to it.

He was sure he'd seen it – but now it was gone.

How was it possible? Nothing could move that fast.

There was movement behind him.

He drew his sword, wheeling Thunder around at the same time, ready to strike.

Vanessa was right behind him. She screamed when she saw Dane's sword flash in front of her. Buttons reared, throwing her from the saddle.

Dane nearly dropped his sword in shock. Bringing Thunder under control, he dismounted and went to her aid.

'Are you all right?' he asked, helping Vanessa to her feet.

Vanessa nodded.

'What do you think you were doing,' he snapped, 'following me in here like that?'

'Well,' said Vanessa, brushing herself off, 'why did you draw your sword on me? You scared me half to death!'

Coming to his senses, Dane pulled her under the cover of the horses. He raised a finger to his mouth, gesturing her to be quiet. He walked forward, scanning the area, worried they'd made their presence known.

Seeing no immediate sign of trouble, he sheathed his sword and made his way back.

Beckoning Vanessa onto Buttons, he climbed aboard his own saddle. They rode out of the forest in silence. When they emerged they saw a patrol converging, swords out, riding in formation.

'What were you doing?' asked Vanessa.

'I saw a Black Knight,' said Dane, pointing to the spot, 'twice - right over there. But when I went in to see, he'd gone.'

Vanessa's eyes widened.

'The thing is,' Dane added, 'he disappeared. There was no trace of him.'

The patrols reined in.

'What's going on?' the first knight demanded. 'Why were you in the forest? You know it's forbidden.'

'I know,' Dane replied. 'But I saw a Black Knight, right over there.'

Half the patrol stormed into the forest. The others closed ranks around Dane and Vanessa, escorting them back to the castle in quick time.

After Vanessa had changed out of her riding clothes, she and Dane found themselves in front of the King and Lord Frederick.

'Forgive me, Sire,' said Dane. 'I didn't realise Vanessa would follow me. I should have thought it through before acting like I did. I had no idea she was behind me.'

'On the contrary,' the King replied. 'You did exactly as expected. Any blame for the actions of the Princess lie with her, not you.'

Dane saw Vanessa flinch for a moment as father and daughter exchanged glances. Smouldering anger filled the King's eyes. Vanessa wore a look of angry defiance. Lord Frederick watched the exchange with some amusement before speaking for the first time.

'Master Dane. You say he disappeared?'

'Yes. It was as though he vanished into thin air. There was no trace of him.'

'Very observant,' Lord Frederick replied. 'I believe you saw exactly what happened.'

Dane was puzzled. He looked at the King and Vanessa and saw he wasn't the only one.

'You witnessed a projected duplication,' said Lord Frederick, as simply as if he'd said the sky was blue.

'A projected duplication is something any wizard can conjure. You simply take a part of the subject you wish to duplicate or copy, and an exact image of the subject can be projected or transported anywhere you wish. Behold.'

He walked forward and gently touched Dane on the arm. He closed his eyes. A thin, wispy green light formed around them, and an exact likeness of Dane appeared on either side of the King. The images stood for a moment, then started to walk around the room, before trailing off into the air.

'You see,' Lord Frederick remarked to the wide eyes around him, 'an exact image. What separates it from the real thing is the image is silent. It cannot speak or make any sound.'

Dane was stunned. The images were exact in every detail.

'What you saw in the forest was a projected duplication,' Lord Frederick said again. 'I doubt Raegan meant it for you specifically. He sent the image to cause panic. If word spreads it will have the desired effect. We will need to debrief the patrol upon their return.'

The King nodded.

'The trumpets will sound shortly. We can do it then.'

Dane's jaw dropped.

'What's wrong?' asked Vanessa.

'I haven't registered for the tournament - if I don't sign up by sundown they won't let me compete!'

'I suggest you go immediately,' said the King. 'Dismissed.'

'Thank you Sire,' said Dane, bowing himself from the room.

He made his way into the city proper, where he saw a hive of activity as hundreds of people laughed and chatted, scurrying in all directions.

The Tournament of Knights was due to start the next day and preparations were well underway. Dane had dreamed of competing since he was a boy. Cadets were in the Junior Division, against knights who'd been in service for two years or less. All other knights who weren't on active duty outside the city were in the Senior Division.

One of the major events of the year, the tournament gave everyone a chance to relax and enjoy themselves, to let their hair down and forget everything going on in the wider world.

Dane was a block from the Main Arena and making good time. Out of nowhere, Fenwick, Winslow and Harrop appeared.

Dane stopped.

'What do you think?' Fenwick asked his cohorts. 'Should we let him pass? Let him register?'

Winslow and Harrop shook their heads.

'Me neither,' Fenwick replied. 'Sorry Thorburn, but we don't think you're worthy of competing in the tournament. Unless you can get past us. Then we might consider it.'

'You have no right —'

'That's where you're wrong,' Fenwick replied. 'The way I see it, unless you get past us you won't to be able to register. Whether we have the right to stop you or not is irrelevant.'

'Not the way I see it,' a familiar voice rang out.

'Me either,' said another.

Turning toward the voices, Dane saw Will, Morgan and Donovan Braidwood arrive.

'Unless you want your brains beaten out of you,' Will yelled, loud enough for passers-by to hear, 'get out of the way!'

Outnumbered, Fenwick stepped aside. They pushed past Winslow and Harrop and hurried on.

'Where have you been?' asked Will.

'I was busy. Something I had to do for the Princess.'

'You should have asked if you could register first,' said Morgan. 'You'll be lucky to make it.'

Arriving at the main arena, Dane glanced at the officiating table. To his relief, Lindstrom was still taking registrations. With a quick 'thanks' to the others he raced across the arena.

'Master Thorburn,' said Lindstrom in his usual disapproving tone. 'It appears tardiness is not limited to your schooling.'

'Sorry,' Dane panted. 'I was - delayed.'

'If you are not at the desired station at the designated time for any event during the tournament you will be disqualified without hesitation. Am I clear?'

'Perfectly.'

'Horse's name?'

'Thunder.'

'Very good. First event for Junior Knights is archery, followed by swordfighting, mounted swordfighting, and should you qualify, an agility course. Understood?'

Dane nodded.

'The first event is tomorrow morning. Good luck.'

✦ ✦ ✦

'I am about to become the ruler of Brindabeare,' he snarls. 'And there is no place for you in my kingdom'...
...'I will kill you if it's the last thing I do,' the young man replies...
A flash of red - his father falls to the floor...
'Father!...Father!...Come back!...Come back!'
He kicks.
He screams...
...he charges.
The young man stops, caught in a choker-hold, unable to breathe.
A flash of light - the hold is broken.
A sword is in the young man's hand.
The young man swings the blade with all his might...
Dane woke with a jolt.
He rubbed his chin - another nightmare.
The young man...
Who was the young man?
It was - me....
It was *me*....

✦ ✦ ✦

'What's wrong with you?' asked Marilena during the morning meal. 'You haven't heard a word I've said.'

'What?' said Dane. 'Sorry. I was thinking about last night - the tournament.'

'You'll be fine,' Vanessa replied with an encouraging smile.

Dane made his way to the Main Arena and spotted Will among the crowd.

'Ready to do some damage?' Will asked with a grin.

'I'm ready. Whether I do any damage is another matter.'

'Let's make sure we line up next to each other,' said Will. 'It'll be better that way.'

The sound of trumpets heralded the arrival of the Royal Entourage. In turn the King, Queen and Vanessa took their places in the Royal Pavilion, directly behind the Main Arena.

The King stood; the crowd fell silent.

'People of Brindabeare, I wish all good luck, may the best knight win!'

'The first events —' announced Lindstrom, '- in the upper and middle arenas, Senior Knights will be swordfighting; in the lower arenas, Junior Knights will be competing in archery.'

Dane and Will made their way to the lower arenas, where they joined the others.

'Cadets to Lower Field Number 1,' called Forster, one of the Junior Marshals.

Ten targets lined each arena. The cadets were in an area to the far left. Dane and Will lined up at lots four and five. The targets were at fifty paces.

'We will score three arrows and eliminate two of you at a time,' said Forster. 'The remaining group will then shoot another three arrows, and so on, until we get down to a final pair, who will move to the next round. At some point we will be left with a final group of ten, who will compete later today in the Main Arena. Does everyone understand?'

There was a murmur of agreement among the group.

'Very well, you are now in the hands of your marshals.'

'Cadets - take aim —'

As one, all bows stretched taught.

'Fire!'

A whiz of arrows filled the air, slamming into the targets with a collective thud.

Dane hit the first circle outside the centre. He glanced at Will. Will hit the centre circle, just left of the bullseye.

Dane shook his head in wonder.

'Take aim – fire!'

Another whoosh of arrows. Dane's arrow landed between his first and the bullseye.

'Take aim – fire!'

All arrows bar one hit the target. One strayed over the top, hitting the butt. Once the crowd recovered from the shock of what happened, some of them started laughing, yelling obscenities at the offending cadet.

Dane didn't have to guess who'd shot the stray arrow. He smiled when he saw Fenwick and Winslow eliminated.

The next three arrows saw Henry Featherstone and Hamish Ingham eliminated, followed by Harrop and Albert Webster. Morgan bowed out after the final three arrows. Unable to split Dane and Donovan, three cadets progressed to the next round.

They were separated and Dane found himself competing with nine strangers. The targets were moved back an extra ten paces.

One of his arrows hit the outer edge of the centre circle, and he was a clear second in this round. When the other survivors moved through, Dane saw that Will and Donovan were still there. One of Will's arrows hit the bullseye, drawing 'oohs' and 'aahs' from the crowd.

There were two more rounds before the finalists were decided. To his surprise, Dane made it through, along with Will and Donovan.

'I'm amazed I made it this far,' Donovan remarked during the mid-day meal.

'You're a great archer,' said Dane. 'Why wouldn't you do well here?'

'Don't know. Just nervous in front of a crowd.'

'That was nothing compared to what you'll get this afternoon,' said Will. 'Everyone'll be watching – even the King.'

Donovan looked mortified.

'Nice Will, real nice,' said Dane.

'What? Oh – sorry,' Will replied, seeing the look on Donovan's face. 'Just act like you're shooting on your own and you'll be fine.'

At mid-afternoon the Junior Finalists lined up in the Main Arena. Each bowed as they were introduced. Dane saw Vanessa's smile widen when it was his turn.

'Archers ready —' Lindstrom announced, 'aim – fire!'

Dane's first arrow hit the middle of the first circle outside the centre. He stole a quick glance at as many targets as he could. They were all better than his. At this rate he wouldn't survive the first round.

He was a babble of thought lining up his second arrow.

Same result. Middle of the first outer circle - maybe better than one or two others.

He cursed himself. It'll take something special now.

Something special...

He thought back to the previous week, remembering how he fought past the Royal Knights at the river.

Focus.

Concentrate.

Block out everything else.

Locking his eyes and mind on the target, everything went quiet except his breathing and the sound of Lindstrom's voice.

'Fire!'

A volley of arrows shot out.

There was a momentary hush, followed by a roar from the crowd. Looking up, Dane saw the crowd were all looking at him.

He looked at the target.

He saw his arrow.

In the Centre Circle.

Right in the middle of the Centre Circle.

A Bullseye!

Smiling to himself, he glanced at the Royal Box. Vanessa was cheering wildly. He waited while the arrows were checked. His last shot made up for the others. He'd survived the first round.

The contestants were eliminated one by one, until they reached the final three - Dane, Will and a Junior Knight named Harris Fletcher. Donovan survived two more rounds before nerves got the better of him. The targets were now at eighty-five paces.

All fired nervous first arrows. Will hit the centre circle, wider than usual. Dane and Fletcher hit the first circle outside the centre.

Second arrows were better. A huge roar went up when Will's arrow slammed into the bullseye. Dane glanced at Will, who grinned and shrugged. He may as well have been shooting in an empty barn for all the effect the occasion seemed to have on him.

One shot left.

As if to prove the second was no accident, Will hit the centre circle, right next to the bullseye. Dane's third arrow was the best of his final three, but it didn't beat Will or Fletcher. They turned, bowing to the Royal Pavilion, and made their exit.

'First Place to Cadet Will Hevenshire!' Lindstrom announced. 'Second place to Junior Knight Harris Fletcher; and third place to Cadet Dane Thorburn!'

Chapter 15
Sizzling Swords

The knights and cadets headed home with the setting sun. Plenty of rest was needed before the next day. Dane and Will were exhausted.

'Hope to see you in the arena tomorrow afternoon,' said Will, waving his sword against an imaginary opponent.

Dane laughed.

'Not likely,' he said shaking his head. 'I was lucky today.'

'No you weren't,' said Will. 'That bullseye was incredible. Especially under that kind of pressure.'

'You hit the bullseye several times.'

'Maybe. But you *had* to do it when you did. None of mine were like that.'

'That's because you didn't mess up your other shots,' said Dane. 'I don't know how you do it.'

Will grinned.

'Good luck tomorrow,' he said, turning off Main Street.

'You too.'

'He competes well, My Lord. The manner in which he beat three Royal Knights at the river was amazing.'

'And?'

'And he was a finalist in the archery event today.'

Raegan raised his hand – he'd heard enough. He paced the room.

'We had an opportunity to eliminate him and we failed,' he said.

Those at the table shifted uneasily.

'No matter,' he said with a malicious smile. 'Everyone in Brindabeare is consumed by the tournament. The rest of my plan is proceeding perfectly.'

'What do you mean My Lord?' asked one of the others.

'You will know soon enough,' Raegan replied. 'We need to arrange contact with our allies in Brindabeare.'

He turned to his Brindabeare informant.

'Arrange for our other friends to meet here during the tournament's rest day. We will finalise our plans then.'

Dane and Vanessa chatted about the day's events during the morning meal.

'What's on today?' she asked.

'Swordfighting. It will be hard to make it all the way to the final.'

'Surely you'll survive the first few rounds?'

'Maybe. I have no say over the draw. I could be paired with an ace swordsman at any point and be eliminated.'

'That's hardly fair.'

'True - but there's no other way. They pair us off and we fight until there's two left.'

Dane beat his first opponent easily. His second was another story. A Junior Knight much stronger than himself, Dane needed his skills of defense and evasion to win.

The rounds continued and Dane, Will and Fenwick survived, making it to the last round before the finals. Waiting to be called forward, Dane and Will struggled to catch their breath.

'I've never felt so tired,' said Will, slumping to the ground.

'Me too,' groaned Dane.

It was as much a battle of fitness as skill at this point. Dane wasn't sure how many fights he'd been in. With the exception of one or two they'd all been tough. The heat was another factor – it was hard wearing full armour in this weather.

In next-to-no-time they were called to the arena. There'd be four left after this round, with the two final rounds held in the Main Arena.

Dane, Will and Fenwick didn't face each other. Dane was drawn against a Junior Knight called Justin Papworth.

It appeared Papworth had all the advantages, lunging forward and slashing in the same motion, forcing Dane to back away and fend the blows with no chance to attack.

Dane was heading for a corner and knew he was in trouble. If he reached the rope he was finished; it was almost impossible to fight your way out from there.

He made one last effort to escape, fending Papworth's blow, drawing back and landing one of his own. It barely registered – but as he watched, Papworth stood still, his eyes tilting slowly upward before he keeled over, falling to the ground with a crash.

Dane heard the marshal announce his victory and leaned down to shake his victim's hand. He noticed Papworth hadn't moved - not a muscle, since he'd hit the ground.

'Are you alright?'

No answer. Dane didn't know what to do. Then it hit him. It wasn't the blow from his sword that felled Papworth - he'd collapsed from heat exhaustion.

Rushing to the side of the stricken knight, Dane rolled him onto his back. Papworth was motionless, his body limp.

'Medic!' Dane yelled. 'Get a physician in here! He's out cold!'

A couple of knights rushed to get water buckets, two physicians came bolting out of the medical tent near the Main Arena and Dane started tearing Papworth's armour off.

People crowded around, straining to see what was happening. Dane continued to shout at Papworth.

'Wake up!' he screamed.

The two physicians arrived, forcing their way through the crowd.

'Leave it to us, Master Dane,' said Levens, the more senior of the two.

Papworth was soaked with water from head to toe and most of his clothes were removed before he finally stirred; coughing a couple of times before vomiting violently.

'Very good,' said Levens, as though he'd fully expected something like this to happen. 'Lie still and we'll get you to one of the tents.'

Dane approached Papworth as he was put on a stretcher.

'Sorry about that.'

'Don't worry about it,' Papworth replied, retching again before he was carried away.

'You're supposed to beat them, not kill them!' said Will, slapping Dane on the arm.

'Very funny. Any water around here?'

'Sure is!'

Morgan emptied a bucket on him before he could react.

'You rat!' said Dane, soaking it up and helping himself to some more.

Waiting in the Main Arena for the finals, Dane noticed the sun was still as hot, if not hotter than earlier. He bowed to the Royal Pavilion when his name was announced and saw Vanessa wave back at him.

'Names for the finals will be drawn randomly from the hat,' announced Lindstrom, leaning over to the Queen so she could draw two names.

'Roderick Boustead - versus - Martin Fenwick!'

Dane and Will groaned.

They were drawn to fight each other. They'd hoped it wouldn't be until the battle for first place. Now one was going to eliminate the other. Vanessa scowled, annoyed her mother hadn't drawn the names correctly.

'Swordsmen ready?' asked Lindstrom.

'Good luck,' said Dane, raising his sword.

'You too,' Will replied with a grin.

'Begin!'

The crowd roared as the four combatants launched into each other.

Vanessa and Marilena ignored the Fenwick / Boustead match, their eyes fixed on Dane and Will.

'They're not friends now,' Marilena remarked, flinching at the sound of swords clashing and bodies slamming. Vanessa was enthralled, marvelling at the ferocity at which they tore into each other.

'Those two are outstanding!' said Fairbrother.

'Yes indeed,' replied Salsbury. 'They have the fire in their bellies, wouldn't you say Sire?'

The King nodded as Will made a huge swing at Dane. Dane fended it off, responding with a savage blow of his own.

Down in the arena, Dane and Will gave no quarter. Dane lunged forward, swinging above Will's head. Will blocked him and returned the favour, swinging across Dane's chest and turning around in the same motion.

Dane came at him again, a quick strike above Will's head, followed by an immediate strike across the body. The *clang!* of sword on sword and sword on shield rang out in quick succession as Will blocked the blows.

By now the Fenwick / Boustead match was over and everyone was watching them, unsure who would win.

On it went. Dane would gain the upper hand, only for Will to manoeuver out of trouble and come back stronger, forcing Dane to retreat.

'They'll take forever at this rate,' a voice whined in the Royal Pavilion.

'Be quiet Medhurst!' several voices hissed.

Dane kept swinging, searching for a weakness; but they knew each other's moves too well. The longer the match went, the more tired they'd become, and the more rest the other finalist would get.

He had to do something, anything to end it - now. It was an audacious move and it caught everyone by surprise. He raised his sword and deflected Will's blow, and in the same movement he let his shield slide off his arm and threw it away.

Everyone gasped.

Will looked up, following it through the air.

In that same instant, Dane pinned his sword on Will's chest.

Stunned by the jolt, Will looked down, then followed the point of the sword up to the hand, and to the smiling face of his friend.

For a moment he did nothing, then, as he heard applause break out around them, he grinned at Dane. Friends once more, the two combatants embraced warmly. The crowd roared its approval.

'Nice one,' said Will as they raised their hands in the air. 'Never seen that before.'

'Had to do something,' Dane panted. 'The other match has been over for ages. If it didn't work I was hoping you'd get me quick and put us out of our misery.'

Dane rushed to a water bucket, dunking his head and trying to cool off as much as possible. Fenwick was already waiting for him in the arena.

'I'll buy you some time,' said Will.

Dane heard a crash behind him. He turned to see Will lying on the ground. Grinning, he turned back to the water while people from everywhere ran to help his 'stricken' friend.

Sizing up the situation, Morgan raced over, yelling and screaming at the top of his voice.

'Medic! Medic! Get the Medic!'

There was some dramatic moaning and groaning before Will was put on a stretcher. Will and Morgan made sure the stretcher tipped over a couple of times before leaving the arena, milking the time for all it was worth.

Lindstrom announced the final match.

'Cadet Martin Fenwick versus Cadet Dane Thorburn!'

The crowd applauded, most wanting Dane to win. Will's theatrics had given Dane a chance to rest but he was still struggling to catch his breath when he stepped forward to engage.

Fenwick went straight on the attack, wanting to finish off his more tired opponent. Dane did his best to fend him off, knowing that the longer it went, the more tired and sluggish he'd become. Fenwick was too fast, too fresh, and in time, too good.

Dane hung in for a few exchanges, making a couple of brave efforts to counter Fenwick's advances, before, in complete exhaustion, he staggered, tripping on some torn grass from the earlier day's events. He fell flat on his back, where he was pinned by his opponent's sword.

Completely spent, he tried to get up. He couldn't move. Reaching around with his hand, he tried to move Fenwick's sword off his chest; only to find Fenwick had it pinned tight, jamming it hard into his chestplate.

Dane struggled to move it, only to see Fenwick leering down at him, pressing it in harder.

'I think you can stay there a little longer,' Fenwick sneered. 'Now the King *and* the Princess know who the real winner is!'

He spat on Dane as Will and Lindstrom arrived.

Will thumped into Fenwick, knocking him sideways. Before he could react, Lindstrom grabbed Fenwick by the arm and turned to the crowd.

'Ladies and gentlemen, your winner, Cadet Martin Fenwick!'

The crowd applauded. Will helped Dane to his feet.

'Bad luck,' he said, helping Dane remove his armour. 'Good effort to hang in as long as you did.'

Dane gasped for breath and threw his face into a water bucket.

'One day,' he said between breaths, 'I'm going to kill that bastard.'

'Don't worry. We all saw it. You won't be alone.'

Lindstrom came over and pulled Dane away.

'And our gallant runner-up, Cadet Dane Thorburn!'

Again applause broke out. Up in the Royal Pavilion the King, Queen, Vanessa, and Marilena were clapping and cheering as loudly as everyone else.

Chapter 16

A Final Obstacle

The next day was a welcome rest day for the knights. Finalists in archery and swordfighting, Dane and Will had competed longer than everyone else and were physically drained. They planned to spend part of the day relaxing with a massage at the castle. Vanessa had given her permission.

With no tournament to distract them, people took the chance to explore the endless stalls along Main Street. Every corner had a minstrel, fire-breather, troubadour or dancer of some description. Everyone was in high spirits, laughing and dancing as they flowed up and down the street. News of Mundool joining the Candahorn alliance had filtered through with little effect on the happiness filling the air.

The royals were in attendance for part of the day, leaving the castle bereft of many of its occupants. Dane took advantage of the opportunity to show Will around.

'This place is huge,' said Will, arriving at the Royal Baths. Looking around at the changing areas, which also doubled as massage beds, this room alone was nearly as big as his whole house.

They were greeted by Lady Genevieve, an attractive maid a couple of years older than themselves.

'Master Dane,' she said sweetly, 'I've been expecting you. I presume your companion is Master Will.'

'My lady,' said Will, taking her hand. Their eyes met for a moment and Will felt a shiver pass through him. Genevieve smiled. She thought him very handsome.

'Where is Lady Madeline?' Dane asked.

'Right here Master Dane,' a voice replied, its owner entering the room from the right. About twenty years older, yet no less attractive than her partner, Lady Madeline was the chief maid of the North Wing. Dane had had a childhood crush on Lady Madeline and was devastated when he'd found out she was married.

'It's a good thing you came when you did,' Lady Madeline said sharply. 'Even though you gained the Princess' permission to use the facilities, if it had interfered with the activities of the North Wing I would have simply refused.'

'You've always been a stickler for punctuality Lady Madeline,' said Dane, winking at Will. 'In fact, I was just telling Will that very thing, wasn't I Will?'

'Yes he was,' Will replied, catching on. 'He was just telling me "we musn't be late, or else Lady Madeline will throw us out —".'

'- because I know what you're like when things don't run according to your schedule —' said Dane.

'- and how angry you get —' Will added.

'- and how we don't want to get you upset —'

'- because he's scared that you'll get into a terrible temper —'

'- and how one time you threw a bucket of water at me —' said Dane. 'But I got out of the way and it splashed everywhere.'

Will nodded.

'And the Queen saw it and got really upset and told you that you had to learn to control your temper.'

'Yes yes!' said Will. 'How shocked everyone was.'

'And even though the Queen wasn't here today, we'd better not risk it and be on time —'

'Enough! Enough!' shrieked Lady Madeline. 'Really Master Dane! You are nothing but trouble!'

Trying to keep straight faces, Dane and Will uttered meek apologies. Genevieve smiled as much as she dared and when Lady Madeline chuckled they all had a good laugh.

'Now then,' said Lady Madeline, wiping tears from her eyes, 'let's attend to the matter at hand shall we? Genevieve, I will look after Master Dane. I think I can handle him. You can attend to Master Will.'

Will grinned. Just what he'd hoped for.

♦ ♦ ♦

'All precautions have been taken?'

'Yes My Lord,' replied the first Brindabeare traitor. 'You can be sure they won't have a clue what's in store for them. They'll be too busy responding to your diversion to be prepared for the real battle.'

'Our entry - it is assured?'

'Yes My Lord,' the second traitor replied. 'I will see to it personally. If they arrive at the arranged times they will have no trouble.'

'Very well. We will dispatch the remaining Candahorn and Pardosta forces the following day. The Thorburn boy – you will see he's taken care of?'

'I will My Lord,' answered the third traitor. 'Nothing will give me greater pleasure.'

Raegan paced the room.

'Hezabar has already mobilised. They should arrive in a day's time. I expect it will be another day before the Advance Regiment responds.'

He broke off, absorbed in his thoughts.

'In a few days power will be ours. We will raze Brindabeare to the ground. Candahorn will become the centre of Valentaland, and I will be the Supreme Ruler.'

'What about Governor Mortensen?' asked a fourth traitor.

'You will take care of him. His army will quickly defer to me, and the people will follow.'

Dane was a lather of sweat by the time he finished preparing Thunder for mounted swordfighting the next morning. Unlike many of the others, he chose to walk to the arena, conserving his mount's energy.

Fenwick came bolting past, brushing against Dane on the way.

'You'll be walking home with your tail between your legs too Thorburn,' he said.

Dane watched Fenwick disappear into the crowd heading for the arena. Rage built up for a moment before he gathered himself, thinking about how good it would be if he and Fenwick were drawn to fight one another. He'd make sure Fenwick got his just desserts this time.

Unfortunately it was not to be. In the last match before the finals, Morgan did the honours, knocking Fenwick out of his saddle to great applause.

'How could you Morgan?' said Dane. 'I wanted to do that!'

'Sorry, but I wanted him too.'

'It seems a lot of people want to beat him,' said Will. 'Some Junior Knights were saying the same thing. I guess they don't like him either.'

Will didn't reach the final four in this event, having had the misfortune of drawing Dane in the same round as the Morgan vs Fenwick match-up. He stayed in the saddle long enough for Dane to reach him before throwing himself to the ground.

Dane looked down at him, bewildered.

'What —'

'Hey,' said Will, picking himself up, 'I'm not a fool. There's no *way* I was going to face you on horseback.'

The four finalists were drawn, and Dane was again facing one his friends in the next-to-last match-up. This time it was Morgan.

'No!' he cursed.

The battle didn't last long. With a few telling blows Morgan fell to the ground. Dane dismounted and helped his stricken friend to his feet.

'That was short and sweet,' said Morgan, dusting himself off.

'Sorry,' Dane replied.

'Don't worry about it. Whether you win or not, I have one thing over you.'

'What?'

'I got Fenwick!' Morgan said and poked his tongue out.

Dane grinned.

'I got Fenwick! I got Fenwick! I got Fenwick!'

'I know,' Dane replied laughing. 'We have to get out of here so they can get the next event on.'

After a short break Dane was called again.

'And now,' Lindstrom's voice rang out, 'the final of the Mounted Swordfighting Event. Cadet Dane Thorburn against Junior Knight Robert Eagleton!'

There was polite applause, coupled with some loud barracking from a few of the cadets. Dane led Thunder to the centre of the arena. He shook Eagleton's hand, bowed to the Royal Pavilion and trotted to his starting position.

He glanced at Eagleton, locking his mind on what he was about to do. This was his favourite event and his last chance to qualify for the final; to show everyone he was a knight, that he was worthy of being able to fight for Brindabeare.

The sun was bouncing off Eagleton's armour as his horse shifted on the spot, eager to be set loose. Everything went quiet, and with each glint of the sun, Dane saw a different opponent waiting for him.

First he saw Raegan, staring him down in the hallway the night his father was killed; followed by Fenwick, spitting in his face in the stables; then it was Parnsworth, making fun of him at the evening meal; Fenwick again, leering at him in swordfighting; Parnsworth making an example of him; Raegan standing before him in the forest, pointing at his chest, about to kill him...

He heard Lindstrom's voice out of the emptiness.

'Riders ready —'

Dane tightened his grip on his sword and raised it in the air.

'Begin!'

Dane charged, adrenaline coursing through his veins. Thunder slammed hard into Eagleton's horse and the first of many blows landed.

Dane swung at Eagleton like never before. With each blow he was attacking a different opponent - Raegan, Fenwick, Parnsworth, back to Fenwick, then Parnsworth, and Raegan...

It was taking every ounce of Eagleton's skill to stay in the saddle.

More blows landed, hurting his opponents even more - Raegan, Fenwick, Parnsworth, back to Fenwick, then Parnsworth, and Raegan...

Dane stunned the crowd with his relentless power and efficiency.

'My goodness,' said Salsbury. 'Have you ever seen anything like it?'

Others in the Royal Pavilion shook their heads.

'Not since his father,' offered Fairbrother.

Another barrage of blows and Dane's opponents were staggering in the saddle. He gripped his sword tighter. He raised it to the top of its arc and saw his opponents on the brink of defeat.

With a burst of energy and a yell he rained down his final blows, knocking his opponent - and enemies — from the saddle.

'Victory to Cadet Dane Thorburn!' announced Lindstrom.

Dane remained where he was, motionless apart from his heavy breathing. Everything started to come back into focus. Eagleton reached up to shake his hand. He heard the applause of the crowd and saw Vanessa waving from the Royal Pavilion. Will was off to the side with Morgan and the others.

It had been hard work, but Dane felt as light as a feather; his mind clear, his body tingling. He bowed to the Royal Box and trotted away.

'Good boy,' he said, patting Thunder's flanks.

'Thank goodness he's on our side,' said the King. 'I'd hate to have to face him on the battlefield.'

'I think his performance removes any doubt about his ability to guard the Princess,' remarked Fairbrother, glancing at Medhurst. Medhurst glowered but said nothing.

'And the finalists who will compete in tomorrow's agility course,' announced Lindstrom, 'Cadet Will Hevenshire, winner of the archery! Cadet Martin Fenwick, winner of the swordfighting! Cadet Dane Thorburn, winner of the Mounted Swordfighting! And Junior Knight Robert Eagleton, best placed runner-up!'

All names were met with applause. Dane was pleased to be in the final, but he couldn't have been in a tougher field. It wasn't going to be easy.

The agility course was the toughest event of all. There were no weapons or horses: fitness and endurance would determine the winner. All the arenas had been pulled down and the Main Arena was transformed into a large, open field.

The course was longer and tougher than any they'd seen before, commencing with a run down the length of the arena and through the North-East Gate. At this point the competitors disappeared from view. Continuing downhill, there were some weave-through obstacles to navigate. Once they reached the valley it was a short run to the turning point.

On the return run there was a rope-net straddled over a large tree-branch before a final run to the Main Arena. A marshal manned each obstacle to ensure there was no cheating or short-cutting. To make it doubly difficult they had to complete the course twice.

The finalists were introduced, bowing in turn to the Royal Pavilion and the crowd.

'The winner of the Agility Course will be named the Junior Champion!' announced Lindstrom. He raised his hand and looked at the four finalists – all worthy and deserving to be there; but there would be only one winner, one champion.

'Ready... BEGIN!'

The crowd roared to a standing ovation. The run down the first length of the arena was a blur. Nothing separated them as they disappeared from view.

Heading to the weave-through obstacles, Fenwick had a narrow lead. Reaching the valley, he laboured a little and Will took over. Dane caught up at the turning point and they rounded together.

Charging to the rope-net it was a three-way dead-heat, with Eagleton right behind them.

The net wasn't wide enough to accommodate all at once, and they bumped and jostled as they climbed.

'Watch yourself Thorburn!' Parnsworth bellowed. 'Another move like that and you will be disqualified!'

Dane cursed under his breath.

'You too Hevenshire!'

Heading to the Main Arena they were still close, with Dane and Will holding a narrow lead. The crowd roared as they came back into view, racing up, turning and running back down the length of the Main Arena.

They disappeared a second time. At the weave-through obstacles Dane and Will were still in front. Fenwick ran hard, gaining ground as they reached the valley.

Rounding the turning point it was a three-man race; Eagleton lagged behind and wasn't going to win. Making their way up the hill again they raced for the rope-net.

Dane reached it first and was almost at the top when he heard a snap and a scream of pain behind him.

Looking down he saw Will upside down; one leg caught in the net, one rung cut and Fenwick climbing up. He hesitated, waiting to see if Will was alright. Ignoring Will's plight, Fenwick continued to climb.

'See you at the finish line,' he sneered, climbing past Dane and down the other side.

Eagleton arrived at the net, bemused at Will's predicament but made no attempt to help him.

Dane climbed back down.

'What are you doing?' groaned Will. 'Don't let him win.'

'Forget about him. What happened?'

'He had a knife. Cut the net from under me. I've twisted my ankle. I don't think I can walk.'

'Well,' said Dane, helping Will get right-side up again, 'one way or another, you're going to finish the race.'

'What do you mean? I said I can't walk.'

'I don't care. You're going to finish the whole course.'

And with that, he picked Will up, putting him over his shoulder. Slowly, and with some difficulty, they went up and over the net.

'You're a fool,' said Will when they nearly fell, 'just put me down.'

'No,' said Dane through gritted teeth. 'I won't give him the satisfaction.'

By now the other two had finished and Fenwick was revelling in the glory of his win. Waves of apprehension rippled through the crowd as they speculated about what had happened to Dane and Will.

'It was too much for them,' Fenwick told Lindstrom.

Up in the Royal Pavilion, Vanessa and Marilena were frantic.

Parnsworth emerged, riding towards the finish line. Another burst of conversation broke out. Moments later Dane came slowly into view, struggling up the length of the Main Arena with Will over his shoulder.

For an instant there was stunned silence, before a loud, continuous cheer erupted, everyone urging Dane to the end.

They crossed the finish line and Dane collapsed and set Will down next to him.

People rushed over.

'Water,' Dane said between breaths.

He told Morgan what happened.

'That dirty, cheating mongrel,' Morgan hissed. 'Wait 'til I get my hands on him.'

'You'll have to wait your turn,' said Dane. 'Will's first, and if there's anything left of him, I'm next.'

The medics rushed to see what was wrong with Will, helping him towards the medical tent.

A trumpet sounded from the Royal Pavilion.

Dane looked up and saw the King rise. He noticed Parnsworth making his way out of the pavilion. All talk ceased. Dane glanced at Fenwick, who was standing proudly, waiting to be announced the winner.

'People,' said the King, 'we have witnessed a great event here today, and I'm informed there is more to it than what we have seen.'

He paused for a moment, the crowd hanging on every word.

'It has been brought to my attention that there has been foul play in this event. You saw Cadet Thorburn finish the course with Cadet Hevenshire on his shoulder; a most noble act on Cadet Thorburn's part!'

Applause and cheering broke out. Fenwick fidgeted nervously.

'What you don't know is how Cadet Hevenshire was injured. Officer Parnsworth informs me, that while navigating the rope-net, Cadet Hevenshire was injured due to a cowardly act from one of the other competitors!'

There was a collective gasp and several mouths dropped open. Fenwick had a look of horror on his face.

'The offender is none other than the "winner" of the race – Cadet Martin Fenwick!'

Fenwick looked for a hole to hide in; Dane felt a sudden urge to want to kiss Parnsworth, and jeers and boos broke out in the crowd.

The King raised his hand and the noise died away.

'I am also informed, that were it not for this cowardly act, Cadets Thorburn and Hevenshire would have both finished ahead of Cadet Fenwick!'

Cheers and 'hoorays!' went up through the crowd.

'So without further ado, Cadet Fenwick is disqualified and sentenced to one month's detention, to be decided by Council. Cadets Thorburn and Hevenshire are hereby declared Joint Junior Champions!'

The applause and cheers were deafening. Vanessa and Marilena screamed with delight, rushing to congratulate Dane. Two Royal Guards escorted Fenwick away.

'Don't worry about waiting your turn,' Dane muttered to Morgan, 'What's in store for him will be worse than anything we could do.'

'Too right,' Morgan replied with a wry smile, 'too right.'

'What's all the commotion?' asked Will, walking gingerly to where Dane and Morgan were standing. Morgan filled him in. Will looked at Dane for a moment, then smiled and embraced him warmly.

'Brilliant!' he whooped. 'But I still say you're a fool!'

'Dane! Dane! How wonderful!' Vanessa exclaimed, wrapping him in a smothering hug.

Staggering for a moment, Dane gathered her up. At this point he couldn't have cared less about public protocol, so he returned the favour. Up in the Royal Pavilion, the King and Queen looked at each other.

'Sire, I must protest at this display of —'

'Be quiet Medhurst,' the King replied.

Chapter 17

Battle Lines Are Drawn

The rest of the day was a blur. Dane and Will were hailed by the crowd as joint Junior Champions and a dinner banquet in their honour was to be held at the castle that night.

Will had recovered a little from his injury, but still walked with a slight limp. He and Dane joined the cadets at the Staghorn Inn. Over several rounds of cider they were toasted for their success and made to recount the incident with Fenwick over and over again. Each time the looks on the faces of the others grew wider with astonishment and disbelief.

'How did he think he would get away with it?' asked Albert Webster.

'And in full view of an official!' added Hamish Ingham.

'I wonder what they're going to do with him?' Dane asked, changing the subject slightly.

'I hope they put him in the dungeons for a month!' Morgan boomed. Winslow and Harrop stomped past.

'I wonder if they'll make it through training,' Albert sneered.

'I don't know,' Morgan replied. 'But then again, you don't need to be smart. You just need to know how to handle a sword, a bow and arrow, and ride a horse. No real brains associated with any of that. How else do you explain these two lunkheads winning the tournament?'

'But who fell on his brains when Dane knocked him out of the saddle?' Will jibed, not missing a beat.

The revelry continued for the rest of the afternoon. One by one the cadets headed home for a few days rest before training resumed for the final session.

Dane and Will made their way to the castle. Royal Knights escorted them to the Great Dining Hall where, along with Norman Primrose, the Senior Champion, they were presented to the King and ushered to their places. Will sat down nervously, unsure what to do.

'Relax,' Dane whispered, noticing his distress. 'It's only a meal. No need for nerves.'

'Easy for you to say,' Will replied, almost knocking his goblet over.

The feast was magnificent. Dane hadn't seen one like this in a while, at least not since he'd been in training. There was plenty of pheasant and boar, as well an array of fruits and cheeses. Wine flowed freely, although the drink-waiters, despite a couple of attempts from Dane, made sure he, Will and Vanessa were served cider.

The usual faces were there. The King and Queen; Lord Frederick; Salsbury and Patrice; Lindstrom, Maurice Fairbrother and Medhurst, and Vanessa and Marilena. Also present were General Silvers and Parnsworth. The talk was loud and lively, with the King complimenting the winners on their performance.

' - and Master Hevenshire, how is your leg?'

'F-fine Sire,' Will spluttered.

'Relax,' Dane whispered.

'And your family?'

'They're – very well Sire.'

'If I may say, I find your father's handiwork most exemplary. Be sure to pass on my compliments.'

'Indeed I shall Sire,' said Will, staggered the King knew anything about his family, let alone to speak so highly of his father.

'You're not inclined to follow his footsteps?'

'N-no Sire,' Will replied, wondering if it was expected of him, 'I've always wanted to be a knight. To serve you and the people of Brindabeare.'

There were nods of approval from all. The King looked especially pleased. Will let out a sigh of relief.

'See, no need to be nervous,' Dane whispered.

'That's easy for you to say. You know all these people. I don't have a clue who half of them are.'

'Let me help you. See that man up there? Dressed in blue? At the head of the table? The one who was just talking to you? He's the King! The lady on his left, she's the Queen!'

'Very funny,' Will replied.

'And the one in the Masterlord's robe - that's Lord Frederick!'

'Be quiet Dane.'

The night wore on and there were many stories and a good deal of laughter. Lord Frederick had them in raptures with a flying tankard and duelling goblets when a commotion in the hallway caught everyone's attention.

'I must see the King, it's a matter of urgency!'

'The King is engaged and not to be disturbed!'

'This is important – he must be informed!'

'One more step and I'll have you arrested!'

'But Feryndale is under attack!'

There was a collective intake of breath at the table. Shocked looks were on all faces except the King and Lord Frederick.

The King snapped his fingers.

A guard ran to the source of the noise, returning with the men responsible. The contrast between them could not have been greater.

The first was Carruthers, Head of the Royal Guard, dressed in immaculate armour. The second was a short, thinly framed man who looked little more than a peasant. Yet there was something about his demeanor that suggested he wasn't a peasant at all.

Seeing the two did nothing to ease the nervous looks around the table - only the King, Lord Frederick and Salsbury knew the identity of the second.

'Renshaw,' said the King, beckoning to the second man, 'what brings you away from your post?'

'Urgent business Sire,' Renshaw replied, looking nervously at the faces around the table. 'Business you must hear in private.'

'Everyone has heard your exchange with Carruthers,' said the King. 'Anything else you have to say can also be shared.'

'But Sire —'

'I expect more from one of my most trusted spies. Perhaps next time you'll be more discreet. I'd be surprised if half the castle doesn't know that Feryndale is under attack by now.'

'Forgive me Sire!' said Renshaw, recoiling at his mistake.

The King raised his hand.

'No matter. Now go on.'

'I've just come from Hezabar,' Renshaw began.

'And?'

'They've mobilised their army.'

Another sharp breath from some at the table. Dane and Will looked at each other. The King nodded for Renshaw to continue.

'They're planning to invade Feryndale. I heard it myself.'

One of the larger outlying provinces near Candahorn, Hezabar had a reputation for stirring up trouble.

'Go on,' said the King. 'Tell us everything.'

'Well Sire, I've been in Hezabar six months now. I've come to know Forrester, one of Governor Hazelwood's guards. About a week ago, he told me Governor Hazelwood had made a pact with —' he broke off, nervous at what he was about to say.

'Go on,' the King ordered. 'Made a pact with —'

'With - Raegan,' said Renshaw. 'I knew he was aligned with Governor Mortensen, but Forrester told me Raegan is also involved, that he himself met with him recently.'

There was a collective gasp around the room.

'Is that all?' asked the King.

'No Sire. Forrester said Raegan believes he can destroy Brindabeare, and if Governor Hazelwood helps he'll install Hezabar as his Royal Garrison.'

The King flinched for a moment before nodding for Renshaw to continue.

'Before he can attack Brindabeare he needs control of the provinces. He needs a larger army and wants to make sure there's no provincial resistance to his rule.'

Murmurs broke out around the table.

The King raised his hand and the room fell silent.

'Anything else?'

'Yes Sire. I didn't take Forrester's word on its own. I had to be sure, so I followed him one evening when he left the province. He met some people. I couldn't hear all of what they were saying, but I heard one ask, 'When will the troops be ready?' and another replied, 'They will move tonight.'

'When was this?'

'Last night Sire. None of the voices belonged to Forrester. I didn't recognise any of them. I can only guess they were Black Knights. One may have been Raegan himself.'

'Anything else?'

'The Hezabar Army has started for Feryndale. They'll be ready to attack in a couple of days. I've come straight here to tell you what I know.'

'Very good,' the King replied. 'I commend you on the thoroughness of your work. It is also fortunate you were able to get here unharmed. You will be rewarded for your efforts. Carruthers, see he's taken care of.'

Carruthers nodded. He and Renshaw left the room. The King nodded to Lord Frederick, then turned to General Silvers.

'I'm sending an advance envoy to Feryndale immediately,' he said. 'They must be warned.'

He snapped his fingers. A Royal Knight approached.

'Prepare an envoy for Feryndale. They are to depart as soon as I have orders ready.'

The knight left the room.

'We must quell this uprising before it has a chance to spread,' said the King.

'What are we to do Sire?' asked Medhurst. 'Should we secure the city, warn the people?'

'Nothing in Brindabeare will change. We will send an army to the aid of Feryndale and offer any support they require. They're defenseless to attack, as are many of the provinces.'

'But Sire, surely Brindabeare needs more security,' Medhurst protested.

'Brindabeare is well protected,' the King replied, silencing Medhurst with a sharp look in his direction.

'I agree,' said Fairbrother. 'A couple of regiments and any attack by Hezabar will be quickly controlled.'

'What about Raegan?' asked Medhurst. 'He could attack us at any time.'

'What would you have us do?' asked Lord Frederick. 'Lock the doors? Close the gates? Have everyone cowering in fear? Did Renshaw not say that Raegan needs to gain control of the provinces first?'

'That could be a diversion —'

'I do not believe Raegan will reveal himself at this time,' said Lord Frederick. 'If this battle is part of a wider scheme, it is merely the first act of a much larger script. Raegan will not reveal himself until much further down the track.'

'It's not like they could sneak in to Brindabeare,' said Dane, thinking out loud. 'Our lookouts would spot an attack in plenty of time.'

'Thorburn!' bellowed Parnsworth. 'How dare you interrupt!'

'He makes an excellent point,' said the King. 'There is no immediate danger to us at this time. The course of action must be to help Feryndale and any other province that may need our assistance. I doubt this will be the only incident to confront us.'

There were nods around the table. The King looked at General Silvers again.

'What force do you recommend we engage?'

'The Advance Regiment, Sire.'

Heads turned at this response. Lord Frederick raised an eyebrow. Parnsworth looked at Silvers, confused, but said nothing. Dane wondered what was going on.

'The Advance Regiment?' the King replied, asking the question on everyone's mind.

The Advance Regiment was the elite attack force. After the Royal Knights, it was considered the regiment for everyone to strive to be a part of. For anyone seeking a career in the field it was the place to be.

'I think we need to show we're not going to be messed with,' said Silvers. 'This is a direct attack on a province. I believe Candahorn is involved, and we need to show everyone, including Raegan, that we're serious about our role as the ruling city in Valentaland, and we're not to be messed with when it comes to upholding the decrees of the Valentaland Charter.'

There were murmurs of approval.

'What better way to show it than to send our best troops?'

None at the table objected.

'We should summon an envoy from Candahorn too, Sire,' said Lord Frederick. 'They will deny any involvement but it will place them on notice of our suspicions.'

The King nodded.

'Let's move! I want the Advance Regiment ready to go by morning.'

The King, Lord Frederick, General Silvers and the men of the council left for a more detailed strategy meeting.

Parnsworth and Primrose left for barracks.

The Queen headed for her chambers.

Dane, Will, Vanessa and Marilena remained.

Nobody spoke for a moment. They stood there, deep in thought. The sound of war trumpets brought them back to the present.

'I need get to council,' said Vanessa. 'I'm part of all strategic matters now - including battles.'

'I wonder if they'll need more men,' said Dane. 'Maybe they'll call us in to service.'

Marilena's eyes widened. 'I sincerely doubt that,' she said. 'You're only cadets, for goodness sake!'

'But we're the Junior Champions!' Dane replied, trying to lighten the mood.

Vanessa smiled weakly. The events earlier in the day now seemed a long time ago.

'Let's go,' said Will. 'Excuse us, Princess.'

Outside it was chaotic to say the least. The war trumpets had sent everyone into a panic and people were running everywhere. There was a combination of those dismantling stalls, those rushing to help prepare the Advance Regiment for departure and others who just seemed to be caught up in it all, unsure of what to do.

'Thorburn! Hevenshire!' a familiar voice boomed behind them. Turning, they saw Parnsworth steaming towards them.

'Get to barracks immediately! You are to help saddle horses and check the weaponry of the Advance Regiment.'

When they arrived a Junior Knight directed them to one of the many piles of swords, knives and shields. Each knight had a variety of swords and knives to call on. They had to be checked and sorted into sets, then placed in individual stacks to be collected.

The first weapon Dane checked was a full length sword with its matching sheath. The next was another sword, only smaller. He held it behind his back where it would attach to armour and noticed how snug it felt.

In addition to swords, a range of knives needed to be checked. Dane handled each one and imagined wearing them inside his own armour. Each was a different length and fitted inside gauntlets, leggings and the armour at the base of your back – ready to be drawn in an instant should you be disarmed.

'I look forward to the day someone does this for me,' Will remarked, picking up another pile of weapons. 'I'd rather be using weapons instead of cleaning them.'

'Me too,' Morgan replied, struggling past with his arms full of swords and knives before losing his footing among them and falling over.

'Aaargh!' he cursed.

Dane laughed in spite of himself. He too was disappointed he wasn't going to be part of the fighting force. That's what being a knight was all about. It's fine to have won the tournament, but it's on the field of battle where real knights make their mark.

Night turned into early dawn and preparations grew more intense.

At last the Advance Regiment, Brindabeare's mightiest fighting force, was ready. Lined up in front of the castle, they were an intimidating sight.

'Faithful knights of Brindabeare,' said the King. 'The time has come to send aid to a friend in need. Hezabar is causing trouble. We have word an attack on Feryndale is planned. We will give whatever aid is necessary.'

Horses shuffled on the spot, a mounting tension unsettling them.

'I consider an attack on Feryndale to be an attack on Brindabeare, and I will not sit idly by while our friends are in danger. I expect you to defend Feryndale in the same way you would defend me!'

Everyone watched Vanessa hand a multi-coloured ribbon to Noel Hawthorne, the regiment's commander. It was made up of each of the colours of the Ruling Elements. Each colour was represented twice.

Unsheathing his sword, Hawthorne carefully cut the ribbon in two. He placed one half inside his armour, poking the end out slightly, and tied the other to the end of his sword.

He raised his sword towards the King, who leaned over the balcony and removed the ribbon. Unsheathing his own sword, he tied the second half of the ribbon around the hilt.

'You are our Advance Regiment - our strike force - do me proud!' he yelled, raising his sword to the heavens. 'For the people of our city!'

As one, the knights raised their swords and replied in collective voice, '- in the name of the King!'

The regiment moved off to the cheers and cries of the people. A resplendent and mighty force, it appeared most of the city was there to see them off.

Vanessa stood between the King and Lord Frederick; the three of them adding an aura of invincibility to the occasion, their images appearing larger than normal in the moonlight.

The regiment's supply team trundled past and the crowd began to disperse.

Will gestured in Vanessa's direction, watching her leave the courtyard.

'One day we'll be fighting in her name.'

Dane nodded, eyes focused on Vanessa, his face locked in a look of grim determination.

'And when that day comes,' he said, 'the enemy won't know what hit them.'

Chapter 18

Envoys and Invaders

Tension hung in the air like a low-lying cloud. People went about their daily tasks but there was no escaping that Brindabeare was at war. The city was awash with uncertainty.

'Surely we'll win – we can't possibly lose...'

'If Raegan's involved, anything could happen. There's no telling how many Black Knights are in his army...'

'But the Advance Regiment is the best we have. If they lose, what hope is there for the rest of us?'

People looked nervously at the gates, expecting, almost willing something to happen. Eyes locked on any rider entering the city, wondering if he carried the news they were waiting to hear.

There were no changes in security measures inside the city but a lot was happening elsewhere. Patrols in the Great Forest were constant, and for the first time patrols were dispatched towards the Highland Mountains in the North and the Unchartered Lands in the East.

The King's network of spies in other cities and provinces were on high alert, watching for any sign of war.

Dane and Will waited for news like everyone else. With a couple of days before training was to resume they had time on their hands to do as they pleased.

Taking Will up on his invitation to visit, Dane spent a morning at Will's house, learning about the latest in sword-making from Will's father.

The workshop was a separate building to the house and almost as large. The walls were littered with swords and shields, some stacked in finished piles; others in various states of completion.

'Try this Master Dane,' said Walter Hevenshire, passing a freshly cut weapon over.

Dane was shocked at how little it weighed. He'd never held a weapon so light.

'It's great isn't it?' Mister Hevenshire asked, watching Dane's reaction.

Dane turned it over, wondering if it would feel heavier if he held it the other way.

'How good is it?' he asked. 'It's so light. Will it work properly?'

Mister Hevenshire let out a loud laugh.

'Of course it will! Why don't you test it out?' he said, tossing a standard, heavier blade to Will.

When they clashed Dane quickly gained the upper hand; the lighter sword quicker and faster than its heavier opponent.

'This is magnificent!' said Dane after a couple of exchanges. 'It has the same power, but it's as light as a feather!'

'The result of a lot of hard work,' Mister Hevenshire replied. 'Made with a special ingredient Lord Frederick created for me. I believe his own mighty blade to be of a similar light weight.'

'Who uses them?' asked Dane. 'We prepared swords for the Advance Regiment and I don't remember handling one.'

'No one uses them yet,' Mister Hevenshire replied. 'Once I've made enough to supply a regiment they'll be tested and issued to everyone in the army.'

A knock at the door caught their attention. A woman entered bearing a tray of food and drink.

'Isabella,' said Mister Hevenshire with a wide smile, 'it's as though you were reading my mind!'

Will's mother set the tray down on one of the tables and walked over, offering Dane her hand.

'Master Dane, I'm pleased to meet you,' she said. 'Will's told me so much about you.'

'Then I wouldn't believe a word of it,' Dane replied.

Everyone laughed.

'Modest like his father,' Mister Hevenshire remarked.

'You knew my father?'

'Of course! The greatest knight of his day. Always had time for those behind the scenes. He'd visit whenever I made something for him. A sword, a shield, a knife - whatever it was, he always insisted on picking it up himself.'

'You're a lot like him,' said Madam Hevenshire. 'More than you realise. You have the same look about you - the same aura of strength that he had.'

Dane was flattered and humbled.

'I hope I turn out half as good,' he replied. 'Then I'll know I've done well.'

♦ ♦ ♦

'They've taken the bait, my Lord. They sent the Advance Regiment to Feryndale, just as you said they would.'

'The request for envoy?'

'They arrived about an hour ago. They requested to see Governor Mortensen, demanding an envoy accompany them to Brindabeare to face the Council.'

'His response?'

'As you ordered. He's denouncing them as unlawful invaders of the city. He said Candahorn is no longer bound by the Valentaland Charter and he can do as he pleases. He will of course weaken his position over the next few hours, before finally agreeing to send an envoy back with them.'

'Excellent,' said Raegan. 'This time tomorrow it will be done.'

Dane and Will caught up with the other cadets at the Staghorn Inn. They spoke about the last couple of days before turning their attention to Feryndale.

'Nothing's happened,' said Donovan Braidwood. 'There's an army camped at the foot of the mountains, but they haven't done anything.'

'What do you think they're doing?' asked Will.

'Building up their force,' said Albert Webster. 'Or waiting for rein-forcements from Candahorn.'

'Candahorn's not involved,' Will replied. 'The spy said it was Hezabar.'

'So what?' Albert shot back. 'How could he know Candahorn isn't going to help?'

'Good point,' Dane conceded.

'Candahorn isn't involved,' said Morgan. 'You'll see when the envoy gets here.'

'You're a trusting soul,' said Dane. 'They can lie, you know.'

'Well,' Morgan replied, gathering his things, 'I think it's too far-fetched for Candahorn to be involved. We can talk about it again tomorrow. I'm off.'

The others followed, with Dane and Will the last to leave. It was early evening and the sun was halfway into its retreat.

'What do you want to do tomorrow?' asked Will.

'I wouldn't mind another turn with one of those new swords,' Dane replied.

'Sure - but I get to use one too.'

They untied their mounts and headed towards Main Street. The sound of approaching horses filled the air. They were greeted by the sight of what appeared to be a large patrol, heading towards the castle.

Dane and Will quickly saw it wasn't a patrol after all. Some of the riders were in Candahorn colours, one bearing the Candahorn staff.

'The envoy,' Dane remarked.

Will nodded.

'Wonder what they've got to say?'

'They'll deny everything,' Dane replied. 'Even if they're involved up to their eyeballs, they'll deny everything.'

Will nodded in agreement.

'It's a waste of time,' said Dane. 'Nothing more than pointless posturing.'

'The etiquette of war,' said Will. 'Even when you're going to invade someone, even if you can't stand the sight of them you're supposed to be polite. At least give them the opportunity to deny everything before you kill them.'

Dane watched the envoy. There were about twenty in all, with four Brindabeare Knights escorting them.

Four?

He looked again. Had he seen correctly?

'See you tomorrow,' said Will.

Dane raised his hand.

'What's wrong?'

'Did you see that?'

'See what?'

'The envoy.'

Will looked at Dane, puzzled.

'A lot of riders for an envoy,' said Dane.

Will shrugged.

'Candahorn wanting to show their strength. How they also have a large army, and —'

'And the guard,' said Dane, cutting him off. 'How many were there?'

Will frowned.

'Four - I think.'

'Four,' Dane repeated.

'What about it?'

'Protocols - remember what Parnsworth said about protocols?'

'Envoys have an escort of four, and an advance and rear guard —'

'- of two each,' said Dane, finishing the sentence.

They looked at each other, both realising what Dane had latched on to.

'No advance guard —' Will muttered.

'- and no rear guard,' Dane finished. 'That's strange. Why would they break protocol?'

Will shrugged.

'Maybe it's nothing.'

'Maybe. But it's unusual. Protocols are so strict. If we're about to go to war against them you'd think we'd be especially careful.'

He looked at Will.

'I think we should follow them.'

'And do what?'

'See what happens. See if they're stopped or something. It just seems - odd.'

He turned Thunder towards the castle.

'Are you coming?'

Will nodded.

'It's probably nothing, but let's make sure.'

The envoy was out of sight. Dane and Will headed up Main Street, riding fast enough to make up time without looking suspicious. When they arrived at the castle they saw the envoy had already gone inside. They tethered the horses.

'Now what?' asked Will.

'I don't know,' Dane replied. 'Maybe I can find Laidlaw, or ask one of the guards at —' he trailed off, hearing a sound from behind him that made them both turn around. What they saw shocked them.

More horses.

About twenty.

In Candahorn colours.

Accompanied by four Brindabeare Knights.

Approaching the castle.

Dane looked on, stunned by what he saw.

'What in the world?' Will began. 'But —'

'They arrived *before* us,' said Dane. 'So how could they get here *after* we did?'

'They're coming from the Mill Gate,' said Will. 'That's not even the same way. But that's —'

'Impossible,' said Dane, finishing the sentence. 'You don't send two envoys. This means trouble!'

'What do we do?' asked Will.

'We wait and see what happens. Hopefully they won't get past the guards.'

They stepped out of sight.

The riders dismounted and walked up to the castle, nodded past the guards and walked inside. To Dane's astonishment the guards turned and followed.

Dane and Will looked at each other.

'Something's up,' said Dane under his breath. 'Something's really up. That's no envoy - it's an invasion!'

Will was about to reply when there was the sound of more horses. Another group of riders arrived. Again, most were dressed in Candahorn uniforms. They didn't hesitate before dismounting and hurrying inside the castle.

'What in the world?' Will gasped.

'Don't you get it?' said Dane. 'They're posing as envoys, but they're invaders!'

'But how are they getting in?'

'We don't have time to worry about that! We have to raise the alarm - now!'

They left their hiding place and ran up the steps into the castle. Swords drawn, they expected to run headlong into a force of Candahorn invaders. Instead there was nothing but silence - the entrance hall was deserted.

Seeing the myriad of doorways and knowing the many passageways leading from the entrance hall, Dane's heart sank. They could have gone through any one of them.

Where did he go now? He made up his mind in an instant.

Vanessa!

He had to get to Vanessa.

'Come on!' he yelled, sprinting to his left.

Will followed. Rounding a corner, they took a flight of stairs and raced down the hallway. They came to a balcony at the end and Dane glanced over. From here he had a good view both below and above him. He was stunned at what he saw.

Across the other side of the castle, moving down a hallway running parallel to where he was standing was one of the 'envoys', accompanied by their Brindabeare escorts - only they weren't that at all. As he watched, the entire group changed its appearance - from the ground up their armour turned black from head to toe. Once their transformation was complete they raced off again. Dane couldn't see their faces but he knew what they were - *Black Knights!*

'Black Knights!' he yelled. 'Black Knights!'

He looked again - he couldn't believe his eyes: Black Knights were everywhere - teeming down the hallway on the other side of the castle.

Where were they all coming from?

He turned to Will, his face full of panic. 'They're everywhere - dozens of them!'

He tore off down the hallway.

'This way!' he screamed.

Will followed, sword out and ready.

Dane forced himself to run faster. He had to get to Vanessa before it was too late. They raced up another flight of stairs and round a corner, bolting past a couple of guards.

'Black Knights!' Dane yelled. 'In the castle!'

Bounding up another flight of steps, they rounded a bend and arrived at Vanessa's quarters. Dane pounded on the door.

'Vanessa! Open the door! Open the door!'

There was the sound of footsteps and the door opened.

'What?'

'No time to explain!' Dane yelled, pulling Vanessa out of the room and breaking into a run. Will was right behind, dragging Marilena with him.

'Dane!' Vanessa exclaimed, 'what's going on!?'

'Black Knights! You have to get out of here!'

'Wh – what do you mean!?' she said, doing her best not to fall over.

'Envoys!' Dane answered, rounding a corner and heading down the hallway. 'All arriving at different points – they're Black Knights!'

Vanessa was about to reply, but as they rounded the next corner - there they were. Dane, Will, Vanessa and Marilena were confronted by four Black Knights. And when the first one spoke, they were stunned beyond belief.

Chapter 19
Defending the Castle

'Evening gents.'

Their mouths dropped open.

'Why the surprise? Especially you Thorburn. You've seen Black Knights before.'

They couldn't believe it, but the voice was unmistakable.

'Morgan?' asked Dane, dumbfounded.

'The one and only.'

'Why? How could you?'

He looked at Will again. It was incredible. Morgan Hainsley - their friend, was a Black Knight. A traitor. How could it be? His mind was spinning.

Morgan was an easygoing, free-spirited, happy-go-lucky soul. Always ready to spin a good yarn, to say something funny to lighten the moment - he was happy to be the butt of people's jokes and stories if it meant a good laugh.

It was impossible to imagine that all this time, through all the adventures of training, the triumphs and struggles, that he'd been plotting against them – *in league* with and *conspiring* with Raegan.

Dane looked again, willing it to be someone else.

'I've had to endure watching you and your family get privileges all your life. Privileges that should have been mine,' Morgan said with a hate in his voice Dane hadn't heard before. 'Your father had my father disgraced and thrown out of the army. You weren't stupid enough to think I wouldn't make you pay for it someday, were you?'

Dane looked at Will, Vanessa and Marilena in disbelief.

'What are you talking about?' he asked.

'Don't tell me you don't know!' Morgan yelled. 'The battle at Pardosta. My father commanded the 3rd Battalion, and when he saw the 2nd Battalion in trouble, he did what any commander worth his salt would have done - he went to their aid! And what did he get for it? Instead of praise, *your* father expelled him from the army!'

Dane and the others were stunned.

'Morgan,' said Dane gently, 'that was over twenty years ago.'

'Try telling that to my father! He's been riddled with shame since that day. He's lost his career, his pride – everything!

'I saw what it had done to him, and I swore I'd make amends any way I could. And what better way to do it than to kill the son of the man who ruined his life and serve the Supreme Ruler of Valentaland, Lord Raegan!'

'Morgan,' Dane pleaded, 'we're friends. After all we've been through together –'

'All what?' Morgan yelled. 'All those times we laughed and carried on - it used to make me sick!'

'So what are you going to do now?' asked Will.

'Always the fool Hevenshire,' Morgan spat. 'Isn't it obvious? Me and my friends here are going to kill you. Then Lord Raegan will kill the King and that pathetic brother of his and rule all Valentaland.'

'How dare you!' Vanessa yelled. 'I am the Princess of Brindabeare and heir to the throne. You will cease this outrage at once!'

Morgan laughed.

'Princess, you think your words are going to make me bow at your feet? You're nothing. A nobody. So forgive me if I'm not trembling in my boots. I only had orders to kill Thorburn tonight, but I'll enjoy killing you as well.'

Vanessa didn't flinch. Instead she took a defiant step forward.

'If it is my fate to die tonight at least *I* won't do it hiding behind war-paint and black armour. You're nothing but a coward.'

Morgan flinched. Vanessa saw it and latched on to an idea.

'If you are going to kill me, at least do the honourable thing and unmask yourself.'

Dane grabbed her and pulled her back behind him.

'How about it Morgan? Are you going to hide behind black paint or beat me man to man? I think your father would rather hear I was killed by Morgan Hainsley - not some faceless Black Knight.'

'Oh he'll know alright. When Lord Raegan is installed as Supreme Ruler, I'll visit him personally and present him with your head!'

Before another word could be said there was a flash of white light, a bang, and a cloud of smoke. Lord Frederick appeared, standing between the two groups.

He turned to Dane and the others.

'Well done Master Dane. I was concerned when I sensed the Princess was not in her quarters. I am pleased to see you all in one piece.'

Dane gave a nervous nod.

Lord Frederick turned his attention to the Black Knights.

'Master Hainsley,' he said, his eyes locking on Morgan, 'you disappoint me. I would have thought the proper course to take would be to distinguish yourself in our service. What you have done instead is cause further embarrassment to your family.'

Morgan lost control and lunged forward. After one step Lord Frederick stopped him with a choker hold. Morgan clutched his neck, fighting for air.

The other Black Knights drew their swords, ready to attack. Lord Frederick raised his other hand.

'I would not do that if I were you. I already have Master Hainsley in my control. It would take nothing to similarly contain you.'

The Black Knights exchanged looks, unsure of what to do.

'I offer you one chance, one chance only, to lower your weapons and surrender. Do it now – or suffer the consequences.'

Before they could react there was a flash of red light, a bang, and Raegan stepped forward.

'They only take orders from me brother,' he said. 'Their lives mean nothing to them. All that matters is doing as I command.'

Raegan looked as menacing as ever, but Dane felt no fear. Strangely calm, he felt he'd been preparing for this moment for eleven years, as though he was reliving that night with a chance to settle everything once and for all. He was ready to face whatever was about to happen.

'You've failed, Raegan,' said Lord Frederick. 'If this is all you have managed to muster you will not get far.'

'I'm afraid you're wrong,' Raegan replied with a smile. 'There are others making their way through the castle at this very moment.'

'I find that hard to believe. They would not have made it past the gatehouse.'

Raegan smiled again. 'But they have. Past the Main Gate, the North-West Gate, and the Mill Gate.'

'It's true,' said Dane. 'Will and I saw them arrive.'

'Be that as it may, you will fail,' said Lord Frederick.

'I will not,' Raegan replied. 'Right now a group is heading towards the King's quarters. In a matter of moments he will be dead.'

Lord Frederick flinched. Vanessa clapped her hand to her face in horror and Dane went wide-eyed with shock. For a moment Lord Frederick was at a loss as to what to do. He wanted desperately to save the King, but he couldn't leave now Raegan was here. Raegan had to be taken care of first, no matter the consequences.

'I don't believe you,' he said with a quavering voice. 'You'd want to do it yourself.'

Dane thought about the possibility of Raegan killing the King; or worse – that the King may already be dead. A wave of anger swept over him.

'You won't win, Raegan,' he said. 'Lord Frederick will kill you first – and if he doesn't then I will.'

With a wave of his hand Raegan sent a Spell of Death flashing towards Dane. In the same instant Lord Frederick released the choker hold on Morgan and raised his hand, swatting the bolt away. It hit an invisible barrier and disappeared.

'You will have to kill me first,' he said.

'As you wish,' Raegan replied.

There was a commotion in the hallway behind Dane - the sound of steel on steel and voices yelling and screaming.

Dane felt a surge of adrenaline course through him. They were trapped. No way forward and no way back.

'It begins!' Raegan yelled, ripping his sword from its sheath and lunging at his brother.

Lord Frederick swung at Raegan, occupying his full scope of vision. Raegan wouldn't be able to hurt Vanessa unless he died first. If it came to that, Lord Frederick hoped the others would have had time to escape.

Guessing there was more happening behind than in front of him, Dane grabbed Vanessa and ran forward. They crashed into and around their opponents, followed closely by Will and Marilena. For the moment at least they could retreat further down the hallway.

'Stay behind me!' Dane yelled, turning to face Morgan. He stood so Vanessa was directly behind him, her back to the wall. Will did the same thing with Marilena on the other side of the hallway.

Morgan lunged. Dane raised his sword, fending off the blow. The force was unlike any he'd taken in training. Morgan was stronger now he was a Black Knight. Under normal conditions Dane would win easily. Now the odds were even.

Will took a blow from one of the Black Knights that almost knocked him over. It took all his skill to stay on his feet. He was in a hopeless position. His opponent was already bigger and stronger. With the added strength it was even more of a mismatch.

Morgan came at Dane again. Dane blocked the blow, ducked his head and swung back with all his might. Morgan absorbed the hit, staggered a little, but was otherwise unaffected. Dane couldn't believe it. He'd hit Morgan with all his strength and it barely registered. Without a way to counteract their strength, the Black Knights would take them in a matter of moments.

Will stuck a boot into his opponent, throwing him back and giving himself a chance to prepare for the next blow.

His opponent lunged again. Will pushed Marilena to the ground and spun away at the last instant. He swung at his attacker in the same motion, slashing hard across his chest. His assailant screamed as Will penetrated a gap between the plates of armour and cut through to the skin.

Dane threw Morgan off, striking out hard with his boot and sending him across the hallway.

Another Black Knight charged.

Crouching in his stance, Dane sprang forward and up, thrusting his sword under his opponent's chestplate and into the skin.

With a scream of terror the Black Knight fell forward, the life draining out of him. He and Dane crashed to the floor. The knight's body disappeared. Dane threw the empty armour off himself and jumped to his feet.

Morgan lunged again.

Dane blocked the blow and fended him off, pushing him to the left. Another Black Knight came at him from the right. He was in a hopeless position; outnumbered and limited in what he could do to fight back due to his need to stand between Vanessa and the enemy.

Reaching down, he grabbed a sword and threw it up to her. Vanessa caught it in a mixture of reflex and shock. Dane nodded.

'Use it!' he yelled, stepping to his right, leaving her more exposed to direct attack.

Vanessa looked at the sword, then back to Dane with wide eyes. Surely not! She'd only ever sparred with him; just for fun, and now he was expecting her to.....

Clang!

Morgan swung at her and by reflex she blocked the blow. She looked in front of herself in shock. She'd blocked it! She'd stopped him! She'd had a moment to react and she'd done it!

Morgan came at her again. Again she blocked him. He was stronger, but she was quicker. She wouldn't last long, but maybe she could handle him long enough to find a chance to escape.

Dane stepped right away from her. Morgan rushed again. This time she staggered, bumping into Dane. She didn't fall over but knocked Dane off balance, giving his opponent a better shot at him. Dane felt a bolt of pain when the Black Knight swung and opened a cut in his left arm.

At the other end of the hallway Lord Frederick and Raegan were hammering into each other. Wizard against wizard; Masterlord and Firelord, brother versus brother. The only way either could die was from the sword of the other – it was their own private battle.

Swords clashed and spells erupted as each sought an advantage.

'You will perish this night,' said Raegan.

A web of red light left his hand, wrapping around Lord Frederick. A ball of white light erupted, filling the void between them. In the next instant the web exploded and Lord Frederick leapt forward.

'Not if I have anything to do with it.'

Lord Frederick let out twin blasts of azure. The first struck below the knee, wrapping around Raegan's legs. The second hit Raegan's forearm, the force of the blast hurling him into a wall.

Manacles emerged from within the wall, wrapping around Raegan's arms.

'No!' he screamed.

Lord Frederick rushed forward, Scarafuse drawn, ready for the kill.

Raegan raised a wall of flame in front of him, followed by a thin spark that sailed over Lord Frederick's head. The spark landed on the floor and exploded.

Lord Frederick spun on his heels and swung Scarafuse in an arc across his body. Raegan appeared where the spark landed and lunged at Lord Frederick, their swords clashing before they separated and faced up to each other once more.

'You need to do better than that,' said Lord Frederick.

'By all means,' Raegan replied, another flash bursting from his hand.

By now the battle coming from behind them had converged on this one. In all there were about thirty Black Knights and as many Royal Knights in the fight.

Dane and Vanessa maintained their defensive positions, unable to move from where they were.

Vanessa continued to hold Morgan off, and the fact she didn't fall with his first strike was grating on him. He couldn't believe Dane had been so stupid to leave her as vulnerable as he had, giving him an easy kill.

The ultimate redemption. He'd kill the Princess, kill Dane, and then tell all and sundry what the great Gil Thorburn's son had done - in her greatest hour of need he'd left the Princess defenseless.

It was so simple, but it was going wrong. *Terribly* wrong. Instead of an easy kill, she'd parried the blow, and another, and another.

What's going on - this can't be happening! She's - *fighting!* - she - *knows* how to fight!

Vanessa blocked the next blow but she was tiring. She couldn't hold on much longer. She saw Dane preoccupied with his opponent, unable to offer any help. Morgan swung again. She blocked it, stepping away a little.

Her mind flashed back to her sparring with Dane. She was in a defensive position here, her back to the wall. Stepping away would be a risk; she'd expose herself, but at this rate it was only a matter of time before Morgan wore her out. She made up her mind.

Morgan lunged again, yelling and screaming. She feinted to block him as she'd done before. At the last moment she spun out of the way, turning and kicking him as hard as she could. The combined force of her foot and his own momentum sent Morgan crashing into the wall. He bounced off, staggering backwards. Vanessa raised her sword, backhanding him in the face with the hilt.

Morgan roared in pain and fell to the ground. In the same instant Vanessa plunged her sword into his chest, piercing his armour and fatally wounding him. Physically spent, she slumped to the floor.

In the next instant there was a crash. Dane's opponent tripped over Morgan's empty armour, giving Dane the chance to finish him off.

Dane reached down and helped Vanessa up. He stood between her and the wall as he'd done before.

'You alright?'

'Yes,' she replied, gasping for breath.

Facing the battle again, Dane saw Will across the hallway, fending off a Black Knight. Marilena was cowering behind him. He appeared to be winning; a couple of swipes should do it. Glancing to Will's left, Dane noticed a torchlight about ten feet away.

'Get ready to move!' he said.

'Where?' asked Vanessa.

'Just follow me.'

Will landed a strike, up and into the chest of his opponent. The body slumped to the floor and disappeared.

'Will!' Dane yelled. 'Cover us!'

Will stepped forward at an angle, placing himself in a position to cover Dane and Vanessa and defend Marilena at the same time.

'Now!' Dane grasped Vanessa's hand and sprinted towards Will. Vanessa followed, jumping over and around the debris on the floor.

They crossed the hallway.

Vanessa was now behind Dane on the opposite wall. She bent down to Marilena.

'Get up!' said Dane. 'It's time to get you out of here.'

Vanessa helped Marilena to her feet. At the same time they heard the sound of fighting from the left. Dane looked up. Oh no! Now there was a battle coming from the other end of the hallway as well. There wasn't a moment to lose.

'This way!' he said, looking at Will and nodding to his left. 'Get on the other side of that torch!'

Will did as he was told, jumping over a pile of armour and putting himself in position. The others followed.

'Are you alright?' Dane asked as Marilena cowered behind him. Marilena had a look of complete terror on her face, unable to speak.

'Don't worry,' he said, 'just go with Vanessa.'

'Where!!!?' she shrieked.

Reaching up, Dane pulled on the torchrack. The entrance to the secret room slid open.

'There!'

Marilena's eyes went wide in surprise and fear.

'Go!' he yelled.

Marilena hurried into the entrance. Vanessa followed. Dane bent down and picked up a sword.

'Just in case,' he said. 'Don't come out until we come and get you.'

Vanessa took the sword and disappeared down the passageway. Dane reached up and pulled on the rack. The wall slid back into place. Will looked at Dane, dumbfounded.

'What in the world?'

'Long story,' Dane replied, looking around.

No one else had seen the entrance open.

The oncoming battle arrived from the end of the hallway. In this battle the Royal Knights had the advantage and were driving their opponents down the hallway towards Lord Frederick and Raegan and the fight at the other end.

For a moment Dane and Will stood in the no-man's land in the middle of the hallway. With renewed energy they raced back the way they'd come and rejoined the fray.

Dane had his sword raised, ready to strike when a flash of light blinded him for a moment. He adjusted his eyes and was stunned at what he saw.

Instead of one opponent facing him, there were now two.

It wasn't just Dane who noticed it. The Royal Knights hesitated, confused at what they were seeing. The number of Black Knights they were fighting was suddenly twice as many as before.

Another group of Black Knights had appeared out of thin air.

Panic gripped their faces and they retreated at the sight of the overwhelming number of Black Knights confronting them.

Dane stepped back and braced himself to face the two Black Knights in front of him, side by side – swords raised in unison – each an exact image of the other.

The Black Knight to Dane's right lunged. Dane stepped and blocked the blow, expecting a swipe from the enemy to his left, but none came. Instead his opponent stood there, sword drawn in an exact likeness of the other.

Another swipe from his right. Dane blocked it, turned and spun out of the way, and as he watched his opponents, they both turned to face him in *exactly* the same fashion - step for step, body movement for body movement.

Dane couldn't understand it. There were two Black Knights facing him, but he was defending and attacking against one.

Reacting to what he saw he swung at the opponent on his right. The two Black Knights in front of him staggered back, barely able to block the blow.

Dane swung again, this time above the face of his enemy, followed by a swipe across the chest. He was too quick. The second blow drew blood from his opponent; and as he watched a wound in exactly the same place started to bleed from the Black Knight to his left.

He couldn't figure it out but he swung again – this time three blows in quick succession. His opponent was too slow, and the third finished him off – finished *both* of them off.

The two Black Knights fell to the floor and disappeared, mirror images of each other except for one thing – only one suit of empty armour remained.

Then it hit him.

Projected Duplication!

The Black Knights were moving in pairs; step for step with one another, the one on the right a projected image of the one on the left. It was a desperate attempt by Raegan to unsettle the Royal Knights – make it seem there were more than there were and take advantage of the confusion.

'The one on the right!' Dane yelled. 'Attack the one on the right!'

Unsure whether the Royal Knights understood he yelled out again. 'Attack the one on the right!'

Another opponent swung at Dane; two swords flashing through the air, but only one connecting with Dane's. Dane ignored the duplicated opponent and swung at the real enemy.

Further down the hallway, Lord Frederick unleashed twin bolts of green. Bouncing off the ceiling and floor, a cage appeared, trapping Raegan inside. The sides contracted, moments from wrapping around their prey.

Raegan raised his hand and a bolt of red hit the floor, knocking Lord Frederick off his feet. The cage dissolved and Raegan lunged forward. Another bolt headed towards Lord Frederick's chest.

Scarafuse shone pure gold, expanding into a shield and blocking the danger. Lord Frederick swung at Raegan, shards of glass following the arc of the blow. Raegan met the threat with a wall of red, the glass melting under the heat and falling harmlessly away.

Bolts shot from the hands of both wizards, colliding with a bang that shook the floor before disappearing. In the next moment Raegan stunned Lord Frederick with a bolt to the knee, the force backing him into a wall.

'I have you now,' said Raegan. 'I've waited a long time for this moment.'

He lunged forward, sword raised. Lord Frederick raised his hand. There was a small *'Pop!'* and the blow from Raegan met nothing but air. Raegan turned around. Lord Frederick appeared in front of him, ready to do battle once more.

Dane was fighting like a whirlwind. His reactions and reflexes were lightning fast, so quick it seemed to be happening in slow motion, as though he knew his opponent's moves before they did. With each victory he felt a burst of energy and sought out the next one. Will was beside him, fighting like a man possessed.

The Royal Knights were gaining the upper hand, and as more and more arrived the weight of numbers started to tell. The longer the battle, the less likely Raegan and the Black Knights would win.

It was one fight now, covering the entire length of the hallway.

Raegan saw the growing presence of Royal Knights and realised his cause was lost.

'This is not over,' he growled.

With a blinding flash and a bang he dematerialised before Lord Frederick could stop him.

To prevent capture the Black Knights took their own lives. The Royal Knights could do nothing to stop it and a couple swore out loud.

Lord Frederick dematerialised and reappeared a few moments later.

'Do not be disappointed my good men!' he exclaimed. 'Commend yourselves and celebrate the way you so gallantly defended your King, Queen and Princess!'

Cheers erupted in the hallway. Dane and Will congratulated one another. The knights started to disperse, some tending to their dead and wounded comrades. Medics and hospital maids arrived.

Dane and Will assisted with the wounded Royal Knights, before making their way to the empty armour that had contained the body of their friend.

Will shook his head.

'I still can't believe it.'

'Me either,' Dane replied.

Each felt a hand on their shoulder. Turning around they saw Lord Frederick in front of them. They were the only three left in the room.

'You have done a great service to Brindabeare,' he said, shaking hands with both of them.

'However,' he added, looking at Dane, 'I think you should retrieve the Princess and your mother.'

Dane grinned.

'Sorry about using the room,' he replied.

Lord Frederick smiled. Will wondered what was going on.

'Don't ask,' Dane replied, stepping into the passageway and sealing the wall behind him.

Chapter 20

Royal Knights

Dane and Will were exhausted. What they wanted was some sleep - a few days' worth. Instead they were summoned to the Brindabeare Council for a full debrief.

Vanessa was remarkably composed considering the role she'd played in the fighting. Marilena was doing her best to put on a brave face.

'Master Dane,' said the King with a firm voice, 'how long have you and the Princess been sparring?'

'Well —'

'Relax,' said the King with a smile. 'I am not upset with you. From what Lord Frederick tells me, I couldn't be more grateful.'

Dane breathed a sigh of relief.

'About a year now,' he said.

'I commend you. Not only have you been able to do this without the knowledge of myself or the Queen, a mean feat in itself; it's proven a most worthwhile exercise.'

Dane and Vanessa smiled, glancing at Lord Frederick.

'And Master Hevenshire, how is it you came across Raegan's trap?'

'Well —' said Will stiffly, 'it was —'

'It was what?' asked Medhurst.

'Co-incidence,' Dane answered quickly.

'Co-incidence? This has been the most serious breach of security in over ten years, and we discovered it by co-incidence?'

'I think Master Thorburn is being rather modest,' said Lord Frederick. 'If you let him explain, we may find the answers.'

Dane told them everything that had happened since he and Will left the Staghorn Inn: the envoys, the battle, and the secret room.

The King raised an eyebrow.

'And how did you know about this – secret room?'

Dane looked at Lord Frederick and Vanessa.

'I found it a long time ago Sire. Vanessa and I used it for a while - to spar, until Lord Frederick told us not to use it again.'

'I see. To other matters. Describe the envoys and escorts you saw.'

'Each group was the same number. About twenty, escorted by a Brindabeare Guard. But there was no advance or rear guard. That's what made us suspicious.'

'That means they were in on the plot,' said Fairbrother, stunned at the realisation. 'All of them. Including the guards at the castle gatehouse, the North-West Gate and the Mill Gate.'

Dane nodded.

'I saw one group transform when they were inside the castle. The men in Candahorn uniforms and the Brindabeare Knights.'

'Incredible,' Lindstrom offered.

'Indeed,' said Lord Frederick, rather embarrassed. 'Forgive me Sire, it appears I underestimated Raegan's capabilities. He outmanoeuvered us. He knew how we would respond to the unfolding events and used this to his advantage. His masterstroke was the Feryndale diversion.'

'What do you mean?'

'I have no doubt the Feryndale invasion was nothing more than a diversion, designed to draw as many troops out of the city as possible. He was hoping we would be too preoccupied to notice anything unusual in Brindabeare until it was too late.'

'I think we were very lucky to put down this *invasion*,' said the King. 'We're supposed to be able to rule the whole kingdom; yet in this instance we had no knowledge of an attack on our doorstep. We will need to reorganise and re-evaluate everything – *everything*, to be sure nothing of this magnitude happens again.'

Muttering nervously to themselves, the Council members agreed.

'However, in spite of what has gone on tonight we will inform the people. We have a duty to let them know. I want a ceremony in the Great Hall organised for the day after tomorrow. Our debrief should be completed by then.'

There was an uneasy silence.

'Dane, Will,' said the King eventually, 'I extend my personal thanks on behalf of myself and the Queen for your role in protecting the Princess. I consider it a privilege to have you in my service.'

'Thank you Sire,' they replied in unison.

'Dismissed.'

Word was out and the events of the previous night had sent the city abuzz with speculation.

'Raegan was in the castle!'

'But he was defeated! We stopped him!'

'And the Princess was rescued by Gil Thorburn's son!'

Dane and Vanessa went for a mid-morning ride to get away from it all. Dane had already been to the hospital wing. Apart from a dull ache his arm was fine.

'It's your fault,' said Dane, walking Thunder towards the Main Gate.

'What?'

'You bumped me.' Dane flexed his arm. 'I was lucky he didn't cut my arm off.'

'I couldn't help it!' Vanessa snapped.

'Relax!' Dane laughed. 'I was just teasing.'

'Well I don't think it's something to tease about.'

'You were brilliant,' Dane said seriously. 'I don't know how we would've got out of it if you hadn't been able to handle Morgan.'

Vanessa lowered her head and looked away.

'What's the matter? I just said you were brilliant.'

Vanessa turned and faced him, tears rolling down her face.

'I killed him Dane,' she said. 'I killed him. I never thought I'd have to kill someone.'

Dane put a comforting hand on her shoulder.

'You had no choice. If you hadn't killed him, he would've killed you.'

Vanessa nodded, wiping her face.

'I still can't believe I did it.'

'Good thing you learned how to spar,' said Dane with a smile.

'Good thing you taught me,' she replied, smiling back.

They finished their ride and Dane took both horses to the stables. Passing Buttons to a stablehand, he was leading Thunder towards his stall when he was nearly knocked over by someone walking in the other direction.

'Watch it Thorburn,' said the young man.

Dane stopped to see Fenwick, grubby and dirty, pushing a barrow of dirty hay towards the doorway. He did a quick double-take, and sure enough, he'd seen correctly.

'What are you doing Fenwick?' he asked.

'What does it look like?' Fenwick snorted. 'I'm cleaning stables. All the stables. Thanks to you and Hevenshire.'

'Thanks to *you*,' said Dane. 'You cheated and you were caught red-handed.'

'Well,' Fenwick snapped, dropping the barrow and standing toe-to-toe with Dane, 'I have to clean your stable too. And if you don't want anything to happen to this poor-excuse-for-a-horse of yours, I suggest you talk to the Princess and get me off this task. Or else you might find something rather wrong with him in the morning.'

'Tell you what I will do,' Dane replied. 'I might see the Princess later, but instead of telling her to relieve you, I think I'll tell her about the threat you made just now. Then she can decide for herself.'

Before Fenwick could react, Dane moved towards his stable, making sure Thunder trod heavily on Fenwick's foot as he passed.

Fenwick screamed in pain.

'Oh – sorry. Couldn't help it.' Dane replied. 'But what else could you expect from this poor-excuse-for-a-horse?'

That afternoon, Dane and Will found themselves at the Staghorn Inn, telling the others what happened (minus the part about the secret room). They were stunned by the news of Morgan's betrayal.

'We couldn't believe it either,' Dane added. 'We didn't know it was him until he spoke to us.'

'What was it like fighting him as a Black Knight?' asked Donovan.

'Tough,' Dane replied. 'He was twice as strong.'

'So how did you beat them?' asked Hamish Ingham.

'Being stronger isn't everything,' said Will. 'It doesn't mean they're better fighters. If you get caught up with the fact they're stronger and lose your focus, that's when you'll lose.'

'Who killed him?' asked Albert.

'Who?'

'Morgan.'

'The Princess,' Dane answered.

The other cadets went goggle-eyed with surprise.

'The Princess?' said Donovan in disbelief.

'The Princess,' Dane said proudly. 'So I wouldn't go crossing her path if I were you.'

Lord Frederick's suspicions about the Feryndale invasion were confirmed. The Advance Regiment returned in the evening after a brief confrontation with the Hezabar Army.

Almost as soon as they clashed the Hezabar Army went into retreat. They were soon in full-scale withdrawal, fleeing into the mountains from where they'd come. Scouts sent after them found the enemy camp deserted.

No one knew whether this had been the plan all along, or whether they'd received word of Raegan's failed invasion.

Everyone wore their best on the day of the ceremony. Dane made his way to the Great Hall and spotted Will, talking with his parents and the other cadets.

'Master Thorburn, how nice to see you!' said Will's father.

'And you sir,' said Dane, shaking his hand. 'Madam Hevenshire,' he said bowing.

'The pleasure's all mine,' she said with a smile. 'I'm so proud of you both!'

Dane smiled, blushing a little as she kissed him lightly on the cheek.

They made their way inside and Dane and Will saw Parnsworth at the front of the hall. He beckoned them to join him. They bade good-bye to the others, promising to meet at the Staghorn later.

'What's going on sir?' asked Dane.

'I've been told to get the two of you to the front. That's all I know.'

The sound of trumpets silenced everyone. The Royal Entourage entered, taking their seats.

Lindstrom strode forward.

'Citizens of Brindabeare. As you know, our Advance Regiment has returned from Feryndale.'

Cheers and clapping broke out.

'However, that is not why you have been summoned here today. There was an incident in the castle a couple of days ago which you may or may not be aware of. We are here today to inform you of what occurred, and what it means to Brindabeare and Valentaland as a whole.'

The room hushed as he nodded to the King and sat down.

The King rose and stepped forward. The crowd was on tenterhooks, tingling with anticipation.

'People,' he began, 'it is my unfortunate duty to inform you, that Raegan and some of his Black Knights tried to storm the castle the night before yesterday.'

Gasps and shrieks rippled through the hall. The King raised his hand.

'And although it was a well co-ordinated and well planned invasion, it was *defeated!*' he boomed, raising his fist in the air.

The crowd roared.

'Unfortunately, Raegan was able to escape, and remains at large at this time.'

Nervous chatter broke out. Women screamed. The King raised his hand once more.

'Furthermore, some of those involved in the invasion were citizens within the city itself.'

There was uproar in the crowd.

'No!'

'Who were they?'

'Hang them!'

The King raised his hand again, dimming the noise.

'Rest assured, Lord Frederick, the Council, the Army and myself are doing everything in our power to ensure Raegan is captured. We are taking additional precautions to protect our city, our friends and our allies.

These are times of uncertainty and times of trouble. We must band together and do whatever is necessary to ensure the safety and well-being of our great city.'

Shouts of support echoed around.

'It was such loyalty and support that foiled Raegan's invasion,' said the King. 'The efforts of two of our cadets led directly to our victory and ensured the Princess was unharmed.'

More cheers erupted.

'I would like to take this opportunity to honour them.'

The hall fell silent.

'I call forward Cadet Will Hevenshire.'

Making his way forward, Will knelt before the King.

'I hereby declare you a Royal Knight,' said the King, touching him on each shoulder with his sword.

Will rose to his feet. An aide stepped forward and fitted his Royal Armour. The King nodded to Lord Frederick, who made his way to the front of the stage, along with an aide holding a cushion bearing a new sword. Grasping the sword at both ends, Lord Frederick raised it in the air and presented it to Will.

'Will Hevenshire, repeat after me. I solemnly swear, that I will use this sword in service to my King and my city; with honour and valour; for the betterment of all living people and all living things; in accordance with the Decrees of the Annals of Creation; and in harmony with the Ruling Elements of the Land.'

Will took the sword, raising it in front of him and repeated the Oath. He unsheathed his old sword and placed it on the cushion. Bowing to the King, he turned to the people, raised his new sword once more and returned to his place.

'I now call forward Cadet Dane Thorburn,' the King announced.

Dane strode forward, his heart racing, and knelt before the King.

'I hereby declare you a Royal Knight.' The King touched him on each shoulder with his sword and Dane rose to his feet - a Royal Knight at last.

Once his Royal Armour was fitted, Vanessa moved forward and stood next to the King. Dane looked at her, hoping for some recognition, but her face was formal and proper. Marilena came forward, holding a cushion with his new sword on it.

The reciting of oaths was repeated. Raising his new sword, Dane noticed how light it was - how *very light* it was.

It couldn't be! Lowering it, he waved it a little. It was unmistakable. It was a light-weight sword! Stealing a quick glance at Will's father, he saw him grin. He turned to Marilena. He was about to unsheath his old sword when he had an idea.

To the surprise of everyone, he placed his new sword on the cushion and stepped down from the stage. Walking towards a young boy standing next to Will's father, he unsheathed his old sword and handed it over.

'When I was your age I dreamed of a moment like this,' he said to the boy. 'So take this sword and keep it as a reminder that your dreams can come true. One day it could be you up there.'

Walking back to the stage, Dane saw Marilena, Lord Frederick, the King and Vanessa smiling proudly.

Dane Thorburn, Royal Knight of Brindabeare, grinned back at them. Taking his new sword he turned to the people, raising it in the air once more.

www.ingramcontent.com/pod-product-compliance
Lightning Source LLC
Chambersburg PA
CBHW070314190726
48291CB00013B/1290